DANNY AIN'T

DANNY AIN'T

JOE COTTONWOOD

SCHOLASTIC
HARDCOVER

Scholastic Inc.
New York

Library of Congress Cataloging-in-Publication Data

Cottonwood. Joe.
  Danny ain't / Joe Cottonwood.
    p.   cm.
  Summary: With the help of some unusual characters in a small California
town, Danny struggles to live on his own while his father, a Vietnam veteran,
is in the VA hospital.
                          ISBN 0-590-45067-0
  [1. Fathers and sons — Fiction.   2. Family problems — Fiction.
3.   Self-perception — Fiction.]   I. Title.
PZ7.C8296Dan   1992
[Fic]—dc20   91-46240
                                                                    CIP
                                                                     AC

12 11 10 9 8 7 6 5 4 3 2 1   2 3 4 5 6 7/9

                    Printed in the U.S.A.   37

             First Scholastic printing, September 1992

To Stephen Gagne's fifth-grade class:
Alex, Alie, Ashley, Beth, Chanel, Co, David, Eli,
Erik, Gabe, Jasper, Kenny, Laura, Mandy, Matt,
Sarah, Sarah Rose, Seth, Sharon, Talei, and Willy

CONTENTS

DANNY AIN'T

I am Coyote,
I know everything.
I know when I am hungry,
to go eat.
I know when I am thirsty,
to drink water.
I have no home,
I have no road,
only the desert where I run.
Yet I live all right.

from a Mojave folktale

1

THE CHOICE OF LIFE

Pop tells me when I was a baby, my mother gave me a test. She called it the Choice of Life. She lay me down on the floor and spread out in front of me a spoon, a deck of cards, a dollar bill, a book, a Bible, a ball. She said whatever I reached for first would be my Choice of Life. If I reached for the dollar, I would grow up to be rich. If I reached for the cards, I'd be a gambler; the book, a teacher; the Bible, a preacher; the ball, an athlete.

She was hoping I'd reach for the Bible.

Pop says he was hoping I'd reach for the dollar, and maybe then for the cards.

If you gave me the test today, I'd reach for the ball. But it's too late, now. You only get one Choice of Life.

What I reached for first was the spoon. Which means I'll be hungry — poor — all my life. That is, if you believe in that stuff. Pop's superstitious. I ain't. I say reaching for the spoon could just as well mean I'll have plenty to eat all my life. A spoon for a trainload of ice cream. I'll be fat. I'll be rich.

Pop says, "Look at us, Danny. Ain't we fat? Ain't we rich?"

And all I can say is: "Dsh."

I'm skinny as a blade of grass. I've got duck tape around my shoes. I don't live in a big new house. Where I live is small, it's old, and everything leaks — the faucets, the roof, the toilet. Where I live ain't even a house, but actually a trailer that used to be pulled behind a car. Then they took the wheels off and set it on blocks and hooked up a water pipe and an electric wire.

We got no car. Not even a phone.

Dsh.

I was rich once. I won a ten thousand dollar reward for catching a man who'd been setting fires all over town. That is, we split the reward three ways, because three of us caught him together: Boone, Babcock, and me. So we each were going to get three thousand three hundred and thirty-three dollars and some cents. I waited months for that money. I figured to buy a dirt bike, a skateboard, a chain saw, a radio-control car, and on and on. Then Pop said I was too young to blow all that money, and he was going to take care of it for me. He said I don't need a chain saw.

Well, of course I don't. I just like the noise it makes, plus I'd like to take one apart and see how it works.

The next day Pop was looking at a used Mustang, trying to haggle it down from forty-one hundred to thirty-three hundred.

We never got the money. What happened was, Boone's father arranged for some guy named S. Crow Count to hold the reward in a bank until me and Boone and Babcock are eighteen years old. Then we're supposed to use it to pay for college.

Maybe Boone and Babcock will really go to college. Not me. When I'm eighteen, I'm buying a chain saw.

Pop got so mad at Boone's father and S. Crow Count, the only way he could get over it was to play poker all day and all night. With me. We each started at ten in the morning with the same number of chips. Soon as Pop cleaned me out, he'd give me back my chips and start all over again. And again. And again. Around four in the afternoon I had a lucky streak and built up a nice pile, but Pop stood up and walked around his chair. Then Pop draws two wild deuces on a two-card draw when I'm holding three kings, and he wipes me out with four tens. Then Pop tells me, "Never — *ever* — let somebody walk around his chair. Kick it away. Trip him. Because walking around your chair changes your luck."

And that ain't a superstition. That's a fact. I saw how it worked for Pop.

So I keep on losing. I figure he'll want to stop for supper, but we don't. I eat chips and drink root beer. Then I figure we'll stop after midnight, but we don't. The longer we play, the better I get — but he still beats me. It just takes him longer.

Four-thirty in the morning, Pop rakes another handful of chips to his side, throws down the cards, tilts back his chair, and says, "There. I did it. You know how much I won off you, Danny?"

I yawn, scratching my scalp. "Dsh," I say.

He drops his chair forward and slams his fist on the table. The chips jump. "Three thousand three hundred and thirty-three dollars," he says.

Maybe I should've felt bad because I *lost* three thousand three hundred and thirty-three dollars, but I didn't. I felt fine except for being sleepy. And I'd learned to play poker.

We went to bed, Pop in his room, me in my closet, and slept until afternoon.

Sleeping late left me groggy. Normal, I like to get up with the sun. I walked sort of shuffling to the sink to splash some water on my eyes and saw something move. A rat. He was standing on the faucet stretching his body up so he could sniff the bottom of the medicine cabinet. I didn't think. Didn't choose. I just moved. I grabbed a plaster Elvis that Pop was using for a doorstop and heaved it at the rat — and missed. I hit the mirror and broke it to smithereens, mirror and Elvis both.

Dsh.

Pop slams open his door and comes tearing out of his room, in his underpants, with a rifle. His eyes are big as baseballs.

"It's okay Pop," I say quick as I can.

He stares at me, chest heaving.

"I threw the Elvis at a rat. I'm sorry. It broke."

He drops the butt of the rifle to the floor and holds the barrel in his hand. He says, "You get the rat?"

"Dsh. Missed."

"You broke the Elvis?"

"And the mirror. I'm sorry, Pop. I'll clean it up."

"You *broke* the *mirror*?"

I told you Pop's superstitious. Now he tells me I'll have seven years' bad luck unless I don't touch it for seven hours and then save the pieces for a night when there's no moon and no stars, and then I have to bury it in a graveyard at midnight.

I tell Pop, "I'd rather have the bad luck."

Pop says, "If you have bad luck, living with me, I'll have bad luck, too."

"I don't believe that stuff."

"You sure, Danny? What's the best that could happen?"

"If I bury it, the best that could happen is I lose half a night's sleep and make a trip to a graveyard."

"And?"

"And I have good luck."

"Now, Danny. What's the worst that could happen?"

"Seven years' bad luck."

"Seven *years* — or one trip to a graveyard. Ain't the best worth the worst?"

"You come with me, Pop?"

"You scared?"

"No."

Pop's eyes flicker. He doesn't believe me. "Probably be foggy," he says. "We could do it tonight."

Just as Pop predicted, the night was foggy. No moon. No stars. After waiting the seven hours, I picked up the pieces of mirror and only cut my fingers once. I put the pieces in a grocery bag, and the Elvis, too. Might as well bury them both, in case it's bad luck to break a plaster Elvis and nobody's figured it out yet.

Pop brought a flashlight. It was plenty dark outside. No streetlights. Not even a light from a house. Pop and me, we live in the mountains, just outside a little town called San Puerco. Our trailer is downhill from a farmhouse and a chicken coop. Workers used to live here when they helped with the crops. Now the old farmer won't plant the fields; he just lets another man run cattle on his land, so he lets us use the trailer. We pay rent.

Pop walked behind me. I asked him to turn on the flashlight.

"No," he said. "You can't see with a flashlight."

"Are the batteries dead?"

"No." He turned it on. "See? Now you're blind."

"I can see."

"All you can see is where the flashlight's pointing. You're blind everywhere else. And anybody else around here, he can see *you*."

It was true.

He turned it off. Now I was *really* blind. Then my eyes readjusted to the dark, and Pop was right. I could see more — a bigger area, anyway — with it off. Pop knows things like how to walk in the dark. His mother was Cherokee Indian. What he didn't learn from being half Indian, he learned from fighting in Vietnam. 'Nam, he calls it. In 'Nam, he said once, you either learned or you died. And he said a lot of people learned and still died anyway. Pop talks about dead people a lot. Like they're still alive, sometimes.

At the end of the driveway we turned up the dirt road. A little ways up the road we climbed a barbed wire fence and walked through the grass up a hill. At the top of the hill there's an old graveyard with just one family buried there, three tombstones, one fallen over. Somebody brought an old metal bed frame up there and set it over one of the graves — to keep the cattle from stomping it, I guess.

I set down the grocery bag and the shovel.

"You can dig the hole now," Pop said. "Just don't dump the mirror in until midnight."

"I brought the Elvis, too."

"Good idea," Pop said, and he sat down, leaning against the trunk of an oak tree.

"How will we know when it's midnight?" I asked. Neither of us had wristwatches.

"I'll tell you." Pop doesn't believe in wristwatches. It comes with being part Cherokee Indian. He uses a different kind of time. I can't explain it, but it's a time that doesn't use numbers. The right time, he calls it. Not the real time, but the right time.

I dug a hole, not too deep. The ground was soft. I hoped I didn't dig up any bones. That would be bad luck, for sure.

It was dark, of course, but I could see. If there's light anywhere, the fog sucks it up and spreads it out, sort of glowing. The lights from town plus the moon up above the fog, even though we couldn't see them, were making light, just enough.

"Who's buried here, Pop?"

"Some farmer and his family."

"Shine your light on a gravestone. I want to read it."

"No."

"Pop, if you don't believe in flashlights, why'd you bring one?"

"Because it's a graveyard."

"You mean, you want the flashlight in case you see a ghost?"

Pop grunted.

"You believe in ghosts, Pop?"

"No. I don't *believe* in ghosts," he said. "I *know* ghosts. If you believe in ghosts, that means you *decided* to. If you *know* ghosts, that's something else."

"You know a ghost, Pop?"

He grunted again.

"You know Mama's ghost?"

"Danny."

"What?"

"Shut up."

My mother died when I was still a baby. Sometimes Pop will talk about her; sometimes he won't. In a graveyard, I guess he won't. He's got a picture of her on a dresser in the trailer.

The hole was ready. I sat down under the tree with Pop, leaning against the trunk on the opposite side.

"Wake me when it's midnight," I said.

I shut my eyes. I could hear the breeze blowing the fog through the branches of the tree with a soft moaning sound. The dry grass shifted in the wind, crackling — almost, it seemed, tinkling like little bells. Downhill somewhere I could hear the hooting of an owl.

I heard Pop shifting his position. I didn't open my eyes, but I knew Pop didn't like the hooting. He thinks owls are bad luck. Owls can see more than we can, and not just in the dark. They can see the future. If one hoots at you, that's a warning.

Of course I ain't superstitious like Pop. I don't believe in owls being bad luck. I don't believe in ghosts.

The hooting stopped. For a minute, all I heard was the crinkling of the grass and the moaning of the tree. The sound a ghost would make. If you believed in ghosts. I was holding my eyes shut. I made up my mind I wasn't going to look. If I looked, that would mean I was worried about ghosts. And I wasn't worried.

Then the sound of the grass changed. Maybe the wind shifted. It sounded sort of slithery. Like a snake. I wanted to open my eyes to see if it was a snake. But I held them shut. I was afraid I'd be cheating, that I wasn't really worried about a snake, I just wanted an excuse to open my eyes and see if there was a ghost. And I don't believe in ghosts. And because I don't believe in ghosts, I don't need to open my eyes. If I open them, that means I believe in ghosts.

Then there was a hoot right over my head. I must've jumped a foot off the ground. I bet Pop did, too. That owl had landed in the tree we were leaning against. But I never opened my eyes. I could hear Pop shifting. Bet he was nervous. Too nervous to shut his eyes.

The wind shifted, and the grass went back to its old way of chiming. The branches kept moaning. The owl kept hooting. I hoped for midnight or the right time or whatever to come soon. It was too noisy to sleep. The same way turning off your flash-light makes you see better at night, closing your eyes makes you hear better. I might as well be trying to sleep next to a runway at the airport.

Hoot, went the owl. *Swoosh*, went the grass. *Mo-oa-oan*, went the tree.

And with my eyes jammed shut I'm thinking, *Hurry up, midnight.*

Suddenly there's a sound like a fire siren. And another like a pack of wild dogs. And a groan like a creaky old door.

I open my eyes. I jump to my feet.

Pop turns on the flashlight. He jumps to his feet.

We both try to hide behind the tree, but we don't know what we're hiding from or where it's at, so Pop sweeps the light all over up and down around the gravestones, and we edge around the tree with our eyes following the light — and there in the grass a little ways down the hill are two dogs. Just two of them, making noise like there were twenty.

As soon as the light hits them, they turn and run.

"Coyotes," Pop says. He switches off the light.

Now I'm blind. "I didn't know coyotes lived around here," I say.

"Didn't," Pop says.

My eyes start to see things again. It looks like Pop is smiling.

"What are you grinning about?" I ask.

"Coyotes," Pop says. "Coyotes are back."

I'm still standing with my hands against the bark

of the tree like I'm hiding from the coyotes.

"You can bury the mirror," Pop says. "It's the right time."

I empty the grocery bag into the hole, then shovel dirt over Elvis and the mirror and tamp it down with my feet. Just as I finish, the last of the fog clears away, and the moon shines down.

Pop was right. It was the right time.

Pop's looking at the moon. I hear him whisper to himself, "I see the moon, and the moon sees me. The moon sees the somebody I want to see." Then he shuts his eyes for a few seconds.

I wait until he opens them, then I ask, "Who you want to see, Pop?"

He doesn't answer.

But I know. It's either my mother, or it's Tater. Pop and Tater were buddies in Vietnam. Tater died there. Him and Pop were side by side, and Tater took a hit, and Pop wasn't even scratched — except inside his head.

I think Pop knows Tater's ghost, too.

We walk down the hill. I carry the shovel, Pop carries the flashlight. He's still grinning.

"You like coyotes, Pop?"

He nods. He says, "You know the Indians never killed the coyote?"

"Never?"

"Well. Hardly ever. Coyote was the Indians' friend. They say back in the beginning of time, the Indian was starving because he couldn't hunt the buffalo. Buffalo's eyes were too good. The Indians tried to sneak up on him, but he always spotted them and ran away. Then Coyote took pity on the Indian. Coyote kicked sand in the buffalo's eyes, and ever since then buffalo's vision is poor. So the Indian could hunt the buffalo."

I couldn't believe that story any more than I could believe in ghosts. But I asked Pop to tell me more about the coyote and, to my surprise, he did. He talked and we walked down the hill, over the fence, along the dirt road, down the driveway. We sat in the kitchen, and he told me story after story. He *loves* coyotes. And I loved hearing him talk, not because I had any special feeling for coyotes but because it was so rare for him to talk to me for so long. Here for the second night in a row I was staying up with Pop, getting to know him like never before. He can go for a month of practically ignoring me. A wall goes up. I fix my own meals, wake up when I want, go to bed when I want, hardly even see him. Then something happens — the wall cracks — and for a few minutes or a few hours, he sees nothing but me.

I didn't know it, but this night would be my last good crack with Pop for a long, hungry time.

2
THE WAR

September came. The school year started. San Puerco is so small that there's no surprise about who's in your class. It'll be everybody who was in it last year — everybody your age or near it. There's so few kids, they combine two or three grade levels into one class.

Pop started drifting. He'd always been moody, but now he was getting worse. Sometimes, the happiest I'd ever seen him. Other times, crazy and sad.

"Nobody *understands*," Pop was shouting one day. Over and over. "Nobody understands nobody understands nobody understands."

"Understands what?" I ask.

"That's the problem," Pop says. "Nobody understands."

"Tell me. Then I could understand. Why don't you talk to me?"

"Because *you don't understand.*"

That's what I call a dsh situation. He's mad because nobody understands. I don't understand because he won't tell me. And he won't tell me because I don't understand.

I guess Pop thinks only Tommy can understand.

Tommy lives over the mountains and across the San Francisco Bay, way far away, but he visits sometimes. Tommy has a car.

Tommy is street.

Tommy was another buddy in Vietnam, one who got shot. He still limps. Always will. Pop got injured, too, but not in a way you can see. With Pop, it's all in his head. He was two years in the VA hospital. He came out better, but still not right. Not what you'd call normal. You might say he's got a head limp. Like, you better not touch him when he's asleep. He might jump up and throttle you. Or he'll wake up shaking. Or crying. Sometimes he says he shouldn't be alive.

Tommy came for a visit on Labor Day. Pop and him sat around drinking a lot of beer and after he left, Pop went to the closet and took out his old jacket. It's a blue denim jacket, and on the back is painted a picture like an exploding bomb and the words:

WHEN I DIE I KNOW I'M GOING TO HEAVEN BECAUSE I'VE ALREADY BEEN TO HELL. KHE SANH.

He wore that jacket all the next day — didn't speak one word — then put it back in the closet. I tried to tell him about my first day of school, and it was like he didn't even hear me. No response. Not a flicker.

Then came the Medevac. Like I said, Pop and me, we live in the mountains. It takes an ambulance maybe an hour to get to San Puerco from the flatlands and another hour to get back to the hospital. So lately they've started using helicopters for medical evacuation just like they used to do in Vietnam. In fact, I hear the pilot used to fly in 'Nam.

Friday, Pop was in town when some guy flipped his motorcycle outside the bar. There's a new bar in town. It looks like a blockhouse — a jail. But it's the only bar in town. Pop was there when the motorcycle flipped. Somebody called Medevac. The chopper landed in the middle of the highway. I watched, too. Everybody comes when a helicopter lands in town. They put the guy on a stretcher, loaded him into the chopper, and lifted off.

Pop went straight home and sat down in front of the television — with his rifle. He sits there all night and into the next day, Saturday; and then when some raisins are singing and dancing, he shoots a hole in the television. Blows it to smith-

ereens. Then he climbs up a tree and doesn't come
down.

He's wearing camouflage, but I can see him. It's
a big oak tree beside the trailer. He sits in a crotch
where a branch splits off. With the rifle on his lap.

I stand under the tree. I can hear him muttering
to himself.

"Hey Pop," I say. "You hungry?"

No answer. The sunlight catches the barrel of
the rifle.

"You waiting for something?"

No answer. He's looking off at the hills and the
redwood forest, then nearby at the meadows and
grass, like he's on guard.

"You mad at the television?"

No answer. But his eyes never rest.

"Last night when you never went to bed, some
rats got in your room and tore the pillow to shreds."

"Hunh," he grunts, which is the most he's said
to me since he shot the television.

This is the moodiest I've ever seen him. I walk
to town, to my friend Boone's house. I'm worried
about Pop, but what I say is, "You got any rattraps
I could borrow?"

Boone looks surprised. "You have rats? Really,
Danny?"

"Of course I have rats. Don't you ever have rats,
Boone?"

"No."

"Never?"

"No. Why should we?"

"Because *everybody* gets rats sooner or later."

"Not my house."

Boone's house is big — new — and the faucets don't drip.

"You could call an exterminator," Boone says.

"They cost money."

Boone's a nice kid. But he ain't street. Seems I always have to remind him about things, like that the whole world doesn't live in ratless houses or have money to pay rat-catchers.

"My TV's broke," I say. "Pop shot it."

"Why?"

"No reason."

"He's got to have a reason, Danny. Was he mad at something he saw?"

"Pop's *always* mad, lately. Now he's up in a tree."

"Why?"

"Ain't no why, Boone."

"Yes there is. If *you* climb a tree, or *I* climb a tree, it doesn't mean anything. But if a grown-up climbs a tree, there's a reason. Grown-ups are *different* from kids."

"Right," I say. "They're bigger." I'm thinking, Pop and me, we take turns being the grown-up in this family. When Pop's feeling right, I can be a kid and act crazy and wild like I want. But when Pop gets in a mood, then it's my turn to borrow rattraps and get to school on time and make sure nobody knows there's anything wrong.

"Don't tell," I say. "Don't tell about Pop."

"I won't," Boone says, and I know he won't. Boone never lies or breaks his word. He's different from me.

I came to Boone for advice, or help, or something. But Boone's father would never shoot a hole in a television and go climb a tree. Boone can't understand.

Nobody understands.

I go home. Pop's still in the tree.

As the sun goes down, I stand under the tree.

"Hey Pop. You hungry?"

No answer.

I bring him a blanket and a can of pork 'n' beans. I climb up a couple branches and hand them up, but he won't reach for them, so I just leave them laying on a branch below where he's sitting. I sit outside on the steps in the dark, which isn't too dark because of the moon.

I wait a long time.

From the tree I hear muttering, and sometimes I hear Pop shifting his position, and sometimes I hear . . . something else. Something rustling. Scuffling. Under the trailer. More rats, I think, but then I hear heavy breathing, panting: *ah-hah-ah-hah-ah-hah*.

We've got big rats, but not *that* big.

Panting. Like a dog.

I sit still. I look in the direction where I hear the sound. There's a cinder block wall around the base of the trailer, but there's a break at one place so you can crawl under. The sounds are coming from under the trailer through the opening right under the window where my bed folds out.

I keep watching.

I hear Pop muttering. I hear an owl, somewhere far away. Far enough that I hope it won't bother Pop. I feel a chill from the wind blowing off the pasture.

I see a movement.

A nose pokes out of the hole in the wall: a black nose in the silver moonlight. Then I see little gray whiskers. A fuzzy snout. Bright eyes. Big pointed ears.

A coyote.

He's sniffing the air. He cocks his big ears. Then he looks at me. Zip! Gone. Quicker than I can even get a fix on his eyes, he pulls his head back into the hole.

I don't move.

I just sit there on the steps by the front door, watching. I listen. I wait.

After about fifteen minutes, he pokes his head out again. Sees me. And yanks it in again.

I wish I can tell him: Don't be scared of me. Stay. You can live under the trailer if you want.

It's my father he should be scared of. Up in the tree with the rifle. But Pop ain't hunting animals. He's looking for Viet Cong. Right here in California. In the Santa Cruz Mountains. On a run-down old farm, on a quiet night with bats flying around and the air getting so cold I can see my breath, my own father is fighting a war.

Dsh.

I have a funny feeling that somehow Pop brought this coyote here. I guess I couldn't explain it any better than Pop could explain how he knows ghosts. But I feel it. And it gives me tingles.

After another ten minutes, the coyote eases his head out of the hole. This time he holds it there, staring at me, studying. Yellow eyes. I study back.

He looks wild. With regular dogs, when they see a person, they respond somehow, maybe not always in a friendly way, but at least in a way that lets you know that they see you, that they recognize you're a human being, which is something important. With this coyote, I could be a cabbage from all he reacts.

After a minute, he eases back into the hole. I hear more rustling. Once, a little yip. I wonder what he's doing under there.

I guess he thinks I'm an okay cabbage.

The night goes on. The moon moves higher. The coyote scuffles, and my father mutters. And, finally, I go to bed. Let the coyote watch over Pop. And, maybe, let the coyote watch over me, too — while I dream.

3
MEDEVAC

Next morning, Sunday, Pop's still in the tree, but now the blanket is over his knees. The bean can is empty on the ground with the tail of a rat sticking out. I throw a rock. Direct hit! The can flies; the rat runs. I leave some jelly doughnuts on a branch for Pop, then walk to town, to Babcock's house. His mother says Babcock went over to Disappearing Creek to catch frogs. I find Babcock at the swampy spot where Disappearing Creek disappears into the ground. Babcock is cupping a frog inside his two hands.

I'm worried about Pop, but what I say is, "What are you going to do with that frog, Babcock? Take it home?"

"No," Babcock says, shaking his head. "My mother wouldn't allow it."

"Maybe she could cook it."

Babcock gives me a painful look, like I'd just hauled off and hit him for no good reason. He loves animals. "I'll let him go," he says. "After a while."

"You have any rattraps I could borrow?"

"You kidding?" he says, like it's a crazy idea to even think he'd have a rattrap. "Anyway, you should catch them live."

"What do I want with a live rat?"

"Give it to me."

"Babcock, if you brought a rat home — alive or dead — what would your mama do?"

"Probably kill me."

Babcock doesn't live like I do. He lives like Boone. With a mother and a father and a house with no rats.

None of my friends live like I do.

Babcock is fat. He wears glasses. He carries a briefcase everywhere he goes except on a soccer field, and some day I expect he'll bring it there, too. Right now the briefcase is laying on some rocks by the edge of Disappearing Creek with a smear of mud on the handle.

"If you had a rat, Babcock, what would you do?"

"Feed it. Talk to it."

"What would you say?"

"I'd say, 'How do you like crawling in walls?

Squeezing through holes? What's it taste like to chew through a piece of wood?' "

"You really want to know? I got some two-by-fours you could chew on."

Babcock looks regretful. He says, "I haven't got the teeth."

"Pop shot my television."

"You want to watch mine?"

"No."

I didn't tell him about Pop shooting the television because I missed the television. I told him because I wanted to understand what Pop was doing. But Babcock didn't understand.

Nobody understands.

"Don't tell," I say. "Don't tell about Pop."

"I won't," Babcock says. And I don't think he will.

Running home, I'm thinking about how I could build a rattrap out of screen and boards and string and wondering do I want to make it a live rattrap or a dead rattrap and how do I kill them if I want them dead, when — what's that? In a ditch by the side of the road where somebody dumped a pile of garbage, I see two bicycle wheels of two different sizes. One is tall and skinny, like from a racer; the other is short and stubby, like from a dirt bike.

I bet I'm the only kid in San Puerco without a bicycle or a skateboard. But now I have two wheels.

I call to Pop in the tree: "Hey Pop! See my wheels?"

He doesn't answer. The jelly doughnuts are gone.

With two-by-fours from a scrap pile by the trailer, and a screwdriver for a chisel, I make holes for the axles, nail some boards together, and I've got sort of a giant scooter. With the rear wheel bigger than the front, I'll always be going downhill.

I try to ride it like a skateboard.

The wheels wobble. The two-by-fours drag against them like a brake. And the two-by-fours are too high off the ground for me to keep my balance if I stand.

So I rebuild it with washers on the wheel axles and more space for the wheels.

I ride it sitting on the two-by-fours like a bicycle without pedals. But it's clumsy. I can't keep it upright.

For balance I add a crosspiece, a warped old one-by-eight, like wings. Now it looks like a homemade airplane. I wonder: Could it fly? I push it to the top of the driveway, start her rolling, hop on.

She leans.

The wing tip drags along the ground, but she doesn't stop. She curves. She's picking up speed. I shift my weight to the other side, and the other wing tip drags, and she curves the other way. Faster. I shift my weight. She straightens up. I'm zooming down that hill.

That's when I realize: I can't steer.

There's a ditch. Bump! She's airborne. Flying! I go one way, she goes the other. I land on a thicket of fern. She lands on a boulder. Cracks up. The whole contraption falls apart. The wheels go bouncing into a blackberry bush.

I lay in the ferns, feeling for broken bones. I'm all right. I may be skinny as a blade of grass, but I'll tell you something else: Like a blade of grass, I pop right back up again after you step on me. Just give me sunshine, and I'll grow.

I pull the bicycle wheels out of the blackberry bush. Do I try again? What was I doing, anyway? I was planning to build a rattrap. How did I end up trying to fly a homemade airplane? Did I choose?

I fix a hamburger, which empties the refrigerator, and then I finish the last potato chips.

For the rest of the afternoon I read comic books and keep an eye on Pop. I'm worried about what would happen if somebody came walking down the driveway.

Suppertime comes. I stand under the tree. "Hey Pop! You hungry?"

No answer.

"We got no food, Pop, except doughnuts."

No answer.

"You fixing to spend another night up there?"

No answer.

Sure he gets ornery sometimes, but this is ridiculous. To tell you the truth: I'm scared. I walk to the store, which is in town, downhill, about a mile. I call collect to Tommy.

"Hiya, Danny," Tommy says in the phone. "What's up?"

"Dsh." You know what dsh means? It means I don't always know the right thing to say. Or sometimes the word I want to use is one that will get me in trouble. So I say the best thing I can think of, which is . . . dsh. Because I want to say *something*, I want to be *alive*.

"Is it your father, Danny?"

See? Tommy knows what I mean. People who know me can understand what I say. I can *think* words just fine. I can *write* them in school. But talking, I don't want to take the time.

"He's sitting in a tree," I say. "For two days. I brung him a blanket and a can of beans."

"He say why?"

"I think he's waiting for Medevac."

"Medevac? Is he hurt?"

"No. He's got a rifle."

"With him? In the tree?"

"Yep."

"Oh damn. Is he shooting it?"

"Nope. Not from the tree. He shot the TV set, though, before he went up."

"Has anybody seen him?"

"Nope."

"He's having a flashback."

"A what?"

"He thinks he's in country," Tommy says. "Back in 'Nam."

"You mean he's crazy?"

"No. He's sick. I'm coming, Danny. Keep an eye on him."

"He ain't leaving."

"Don't let anybody near him. Don't let anybody get in sight of him."

"You think he'd shoot somebody?"

"I don't want to find out. Can you keep people clear of him?"

"Nobody comes here."

I walk back to the trailer in the dark. On the ground in front of the hole where I saw the coyote yesterday, I leave half of a jelly doughnut. Just in case he comes back.

Then I sit on the front steps and wait for Tommy. I know it takes about two hours for him to drive here.

Crickets chirp. The moon rises over the trees. I hear a cow bellowing like she's lost and lonely and scared. And then I hear a bump underneath the trailer.

He's there!

A head pokes out of the hole. The nose sniffs. Of course he smells me, but he doesn't care. He knew I lived here when he first came to the trailer. Why is he here? Does he know he's safe with me? Does he think I'm a coyote, too? Did Pop send him?

Coyote's out. He stops to smell the doughnut. A coyote's nose can smell a hunter a mile away. Pop told me so. Back in Oklahoma where he grew up, he says all the ranchers shoot every coyote they can find, and then they hang them up on barbed wire fences so the other coyotes will see them and stay away. Which doesn't work. Pop says there's more coyotes today than there were before the white man came to America.

One time I asked Pop, "Did you shoot coyotes, too?"

He said, "No. Never."

I asked him why.

Pop said, "Because I'm Indian."

"You're half Indian, Pop. What about the Irish half? Why do you love coyotes?"

And Pop said, "Because the coyote was here first. This is his land, not ours."

Coyote's smarter than us, anyway. He's got better ears, better eyes, better nose. And he can smell me on that doughnut.

He doesn't eat it. Not even a nibble. Instead, he cocks his leg and squirts it. Drenches it. Coyote pee smells like solid ammonia. It pinches my nose and makes my eyes water.

Coyote trots away.

Well, same to you, fella.

Did he think it was poison? Why would he come under my home, but not take my food? I start to follow where he's going with my eyes when something else comes out from the hole.

Another coyote!

Must be a he and a she.

The second coyote checks out the doughnut and then steps daintily around it. This coyote is smaller. It has to be the female.

They walk up the hill, but not on the dirt trail that I call the driveway. Suddenly they stop. They cock their ears toward the ground.

A coyote's ear can hear a mouse running in a tunnel under the earth. That's what Pop says. A coyote can hear a beetle walking on a blade of grass.

The bigger coyote starts digging with his paws. Every once in a while he sticks his nose in the hole and sniffs — a deep, rattling sniff and then a snort like he's blowing the dirt out of his nose. He must have found a tunnel. Probably a ground squirrel. The smaller coyote goes searching around in the grass nearby. Then she stops, head down. She must have found the back door. She crouches. The male keeps digging. And sniffing. He's digging closer and closer to where his partner is crouching.

Suddenly something comes skittering out the other hole — the back door. The she coyote leaps from her crouch, stabs with her paws.

Caught.

She lowers her head and snaps her teeth.

Killed.

She picks it up in her jaws and shakes it just to make sure it's dead.

Then they trot off to some bushes where I can't see. But I know what they're doing: eating. Sharing.

Pop says coyotes mate for life.

And suddenly Tommy's crouching on the ground next to me on the steps.

"Hi, Danny," he whispers.

I fly up off the steps. He scares me, sneaking up like that.

"Hey, take it easy," he says.

"How'd you get here?" I didn't see his headlights come down the driveway or hear him park anywhere, and I sure didn't see him walk up to the trailer. He's wearing camouflage, just like Pop. Tommy learned how to be sneaky in the army. Now he builds boats.

"I parked up on the road," Tommy says. "Came around back. Didn't want to spook your old man."

"You spooked *me* pretty good."

"I got to take him to the hospital."

"How long?"

"A week, maybe. Who's going to take care of you?"

"I've got a friend. Two friends."

"You're going to stay at their house?"

"Sort of."

Tommy stands up. "Hey Tomahawk!" he shouts.

For a few moments there's silence. Even the muttering stops.

Then I hear my father's voice: "That you, Squirtgun?"

"We gotta evacuate," Tommy says.

"Medevac never showed," Pop says.

"Ain't gonna show. Come on down. We gotta leg it out to the road."

Pop climbs down. Standing next to Tommy, he looks small and skinny — like me. I can't get a fix on his eyes.

"Gimme the gun," Tommy says.

"What for?"

"Because I'm walkin' point, and I got no gun."

My father hesitates. Then he hands Tommy the rifle. And I let out a sigh of relief.

"Ready?" Tommy says.

"Ready."

"Let's move."

Tommy walks in front, with his limp, holding the rifle in both hands. Pop walks ten feet behind, looking around, nervous, like he's haunted. Like he sees ghosts. They go up the hill and out of sight.

I go to bed. After a while, I hear rustling sounds from under the floor. Snuffling. Scuffling.

I ain't alone. I got two coyotes — two friends — staying at my house. Or, like I told Tommy, I'm staying at theirs. The moon shines through the window right into my eyes.

4
BIG AL

I wake with a shout. I had a bad dream. Never mind what it was about. Dreams can't hurt me — not when I'm awake.

My shirt is plastered wet with sweat against my chest. I'm panting like after a run. The sun is up. I swing out of bed.

First thing, I check my father's bedroom. Nothing has changed: The sheets are on the floor. There's a big pile of clothes on the bed with shreds of foam where the rats tore the pillow to pieces. Beer cans on top of drawers. A picture of my mother in her wedding dress — white dress, pretty brown skin, big smile, white teeth, burning brown eyes.

What did I expect? That he'd sneak home in the middle of the night and be there sleeping when I got up?

Maybe. Pop's like that.

If he was here, he'd be yelling at me for opening his door and waking him up. Then he'd ask me to bring him a doughnut and make him a cup of coffee. I'd like that.

When I woke him, he used to jump from the bed and grab the rifle and look out at me with eyes like marbles. And I'd say, "It's me, Pop. Danny. Put down the gun." And the eyes would come to life, and he'd put down the gun.

When I didn't wake him, it could be worse. Sleeping, he'd scream. He'd sweat. He'd shake. I'd ask him what he dreamed, and he'd say, "You don't understand."

For breakfast I eat half a jelly doughnut, which is the end of the box. I check out the half doughnut by the coyote hole, peed on, now crawling with bugs. I wish I'd kept it. Coyotes didn't want it. Come to think of it, neither did the rats.

I bet the coyotes *caught* the rats. That's what all the scuffling was about.

I drink a Pepsi — the last Pepsi.

I'm still hungry. I search the kitchen. I find half a box of Bisquick with the corner chewed and ratdsh inside. There's two six-packs of Coors, but I ain't *that* desperate. There's a jar of mustard and a plastic squeeze-bottle of catsup. Salt. Wesson Oil. Coffee. Sugar.

In a drawer way back in the rear under some

books of matches, I find an old Easter egg. I dyed it myself, half a year ago.

I crack it on the side of a shelf.

Stink-bomb!

I run to the door and heave that egg as far from the trailer as I can. Phew. The fact is: We're plumb out of food. Since Pop was in a tree for two days, he didn't walk down to the store.

I could stop at the store on my way home from school and buy something for dinner. If I had money.

I search the trailer. In an ashtray from Harrah's Lake Tahoe I find one nickel.

What kind of dinner could I buy for five cents?

At least I know I'll get a hot lunch at school. At the beginning of the year they send home a form, and my Pop fills it out, and I bring it back, and they give me free lunch. There's no seconds, and the food ain't great, but it's there and it's free, for me. Most of the other kids have to pay. Some bring their own lunches — like Babcock.

At school I see Babcock with his briefcase. "Hey, Babcock, what's in that briefcase?"

"Stuff," he says. "Lots of stuff."

"Your lunch?" Because food is on my mind. And as I say "lunch," my stomach starts to growl.

"No," Babcock says. "No lunch. Unfortunately."

"What's in there? Money?"

"Nope."

"Rocks?" Because he collects rocks.

"Nope."

"Dragonflies?" Because he talks to dragonflies.

"Nope. It would kill a dragonfly to put it in a briefcase."

"Don't you collect dead dragonflies?"

"I'd *never* kill a dragonfly."

"What if you found a dead one?"

"Nope. They aren't even pretty when they're dead. All the color just drains right out of them. You can see it go. In a few minutes, it's gone." Babcock looks off at the sky, dreamy. He says, "The color is their soul."

"You Catholic?"

"Nope." Babcock looks back at me. "You, Danny?"

"My mother was."

"Wasn't she from Mexico?"

"Mazatlán."

"And your father's white, isn't he?"

"Half Indian. Half Irish. So that makes me one-third Indian, one-third Irish, and one-third Mexican."

"Not exactly," Babcock says, smiling.

"What does it make me, then?"

"Brown."

Babcock is black. Most of the town is white. Some Oriental. We've got a teacher who's black. One girl, Geraldine, doesn't exactly look white. I don't know what she is.

"Catch any rats?" Babcock asks.

"They're gone."

"What did you do? Get a cat?"

"Nope. Coyote."

"Really?"

"Two. They just showed up and caught all the rats."

"I didn't know there were any coyotes around here."

"They came back. Like ghosts."

Boone comes over to join Babcock and me standing in the schoolyard. My stomach growls again. Then to my surprise I hear another growl, and it isn't me.

Boone looks at Babcock and me. "Whose stomach is growling?" he asks.

"Mine," I say.

"Mine," Babcock says.

"Don't you guys eat breakfast?" Boone asks.

"We're on a diet," Babcock says.

"Danny, you don't need a diet," Boone says. "You're already skinny as — skinny as — um — "

"Grass," I say.

"No, not Danny. He's not on a diet," Babcock says. "I mean we. My family. Mom and Dad and me. It's my father's idea. He says he can't lose weight if we keep all our good food around. He says we all need to lose some. His doctor ordered him on a diet because of his heart. We get this powder, and we mix it with water in a blender, and we drink it. He's lost three pounds already. And my mom's lost two."

"And you?" Boone asks.

"I cheated. I spent my allowance on cookies. It got me through the weekend. But now I'm out of money. And all I've got for lunch is a thermos full of diet drink."

"Nuts," I say. "I was hoping to mooch off your lunch."

"I was hoping to mooch off yours," Babcock says.

"Why are you so hungry, Danny?" Boone asks.

"There's no food. Pop's gone. He's in the veterans' hospital."

"He's sick?" Boone asks.

"Don't tell. Promise?"

"I'll tell my parents. You can stay with us."

"DON'T TELL!"

"Why not?"

"The Home. They might send me to the Home."

"I don't think they'd do that," Boone says.

"They might. I can't take the chance."

"They wouldn't."

"What home?" Babcock asks.

"The other planet," Boone says. "Where Danny comes from."

"What planet?" Babcock asks.

I try to explain to Babcock. You see, Boone thinks I come from another planet. Not *really*, of course, but what he means is, I didn't grow up the same way as Boone and Babcock with a mother and a

father and good plumbing and no rats. Since my
mother died when I was a baby, when Pop was in
the VA hospital I had to go live with a bunch of
other kids who didn't have parents, either. The
meanest, toughest, sickest bunch of kids you ever
saw. They had a time after lights out called Torture
Time. There was stuff went on in the showers you
would not believe. One guy named Big Al — I saw
him break a kid's arm. And then *laugh*. Big Al tried
to bite off my *ear*. I could show you the scar. It
was a Catholic home called The Miracle, and the
miracle was that I came out alive. I had to fight for
it — fight for my life. And that's where I learned
street. Now I live in the country in the middle of a
bunch of cows. Actually, I like it. But I'm still street.
Once you're street, you *stay* street for the rest of
your life.

"I'm older, now," I say. "I can take care of myself.
And I'll run away before I'll go back *there*."

"You could stay with us," Boone says. "I really
don't think my parents would send you to the
Home."

"No. Don't tell."

They might let me stay with them. *But they might
not.* The best that could happen is that I get to stay
with them. The worst is, they might say no. They
might say I have to go to the Home.

The best ain't worth the worst. That's how Pop
would figure it, and that's how I figure it, too.
Boone's family wouldn't understand.

Nobody understands.

When I think of The Miracle, I get this cold feeling in my gut, and a wall goes up in my brain shutting off every thought but one: *Keep me out of that place.*

So that's my choice. For once, I know I'm choosing, and here it is: I'm telling *nobody* my father's gone. Maybe I shouldn't have told Boone and Babcock, but they're my best friends and they'd find out anyway. But nobody else. So nobody can send me away. I can survive by myself. Even when Pop's here, sometimes it's like he's gone, anyway. I'm used to it.

Call me this name: Danny Street.

5
NOODLEDOODS
AND
SUCKING SLIME

After school I stay for soccer practice.

Last year our team had exactly eleven players. This year, one kid moved away, so we only have ten. Which means we'll probably lose every game because we're short one position. In San Puerco, we use every kid in town, even if they're practically *cripples*. The teams we play against seem to use only the best players, plus they have subs to keep them fresh. We practice in San Puerco, but we play all our games over the hill — an hour's drive — in the suburbs where the other teams live. They refuse to drive here. Pop says they're scared of the mountains. They think everybody who lives here is crazy. And, Pop says, they're right — that's why he likes it here.

Walt, our coach, brought our new uniforms. He pulls them out of the bag and says, "Our color this year is . . . um . . ." He scratches his beard.

The shirts look like a disaster at the factory. Like the dyer couldn't make up his mind. They are sort of a silvery yellow-green. Like the trail left behind by a slug.

"Slime!" Geraldine shouts.

Geraldine's tall. She's a girl. Great player. With a huge ball of curly hair on her head. We call her Hairball.

"That can be our new name!" Geraldine the Hairball says. "The San Puerco Slime."

"Oh my God," Walt says. When he's worried or upset, he starts pulling on the gray hairs in his beard. Right now, he starts pulling. He says, "Am I supposed to stand on the sideline yelling, 'Let's go Slime'?"

"Yeah," Geraldine says. "That'll be *great.*"

"Look," Walt says, "I know the color sucks, but — "

"That's it!" Geraldine says. "That's even better. The *Sucking Slime.*"

Walt looks sick.

Boone says, "I have an idea. We could call ourselves The Macintoshes."

"Why?" Hairball says. "A Macintosh is an apple. It's red."

"No," Boone says. "It's a computer. It's gray. My dad's got one."

"Those uni's aren't gray," Geraldine says. "They're *puke*."

Boone's my friend. He ain't street, but he's a nice kid. Something you have to understand about Boone: If he offers you half of his cookie, you don't have to check to see who got the bigger half. It'll be even. He thinks — he actually believes — everything should be fair. It's weird. It takes some getting used to. But still, even if Boone is my friend, and he's fair, and he's a nice guy, I have to agree with Geraldine. Macintosh is a dumb idea.

Then Dylan speaks up. He's the best dresser on the team. He always carries a comb in his back pocket. "But we should have a name that's *positive*," Dylan says. "Maybe Boone was on the right track with computers. How about the Floppy Disks?"

Geraldine doubles over, laughing.

Dylan shrinks back. He actually looks shorter when she laughs at him. And sadder. He'll do anything to impress Geraldine. She ignores him.

Then Babcock steps forward. He's the only kid on the team who wears long pants to practice. Maybe because he's fat. Not that we'd ever make fun of him. He doesn't look like an athlete, but he's a terrific goalie. And you better not pick a fight with him, either. He'll sit on you.

Babcock pushes the glasses up on his nose. He says, "Why don't we just keep the same name we had last year: The Thunderbolts."

"Good idea," Walt says. "There's no law that says we have to change names every year."

"Thunderbolts. That's *old*," Geraldine says, patting her hair.

I say, "What about the Pizza? It's sort of the color of cheese." Food is on my mind. What would I do for dinner?

"Moldy cheese, maybe," Hairball says. "What's green about pizza?"

"Peppers," I say.

"I mean *really*, Danny. Do you want to be named Pizza?"

"Dsh."

When Geraldine makes up her mind about something, there's no changing her.

"Let's put it to a vote," Walt says. "Who's for Macintosh?"

Only Boone raises his hand.

Walt frowns. "Who's for Floppy Disks?"

Geraldine smirks.

Nobody, not even Dylan, raises a hand.

"Thunderbolts?"

Babcock raises his hand.

"Pizza?"

Nobody. Not even me. I have to admit, it was a dsh idea. I was just hungry.

"Anybody want to nominate a new name?" Walt asks. He's tugging on his beard. Tugging hard.

Nobody speaks.

Finally, almost strangling on the word, Walt says, "Slime?"

"*Sucking* Slime," Geraldine says.

"Sucking Slime," Walt says, curling his lip. "Who votes for being the laughingstock of the league?"

Nine hands shoot up. Including Dylan's. And mine.

"Sucking Slime it is," Walt says. "Great galloping banana slugs. This is the last year I coach soccer."

He's been saying that for three years now.

The soccer fields in San Puerco are cut into a hillside. Everything is cut into a hillside in San Puerco because the town is halfway up a mountain. We use the upper field at school, while another team for little kids plays on the lower field. We run drills or play scrimmages while Walt tries to teach us what we're doing right and wrong. Mostly wrong.

Sometimes while we're practicing I look down at the little kids and see one standing on her head, while another is running in circles and another is stuffing the ball under his shirt. I mean, we're playing soccer, and they're having recess.

The little kids' coach is Boone's father. He doesn't seem to know much about the game. Or about how to get a six-year-old to pay attention. But then, does anybody know how to get a six-year-old to pay attention? Boone's little sister, Clover, is on the team. Even she doesn't listen to her father. She spends most of her time turning cart-wheels on the grass.

Boone says they played their first game last week and lost fourteen to nothing. He also says most of them didn't even know they lost the game. He's not even sure they knew that they *played* a game.

They voted on a name for their team, too. They're the Noodledoods.

About halfway through practice, Mr. Barnaby, Boone's father, comes over to talk to Walt. Then Walt calls the team together.

"Listen, Slime Suckers," he says, "Mr. Barnaby needs a little help coaching his team. He thinks the kids will learn better if some big kids show them what to do. And I know he's right. Anybody want to be an assistant coach?"

"No way," Dylan says. "No way, baby."

"I will," Geraldine says.

"Me, too," Dylan says. "I'll help."

Walt gives Dylan a funny look. Walt is Dylan's father.

"Okay, that's two," Walt says. "Anybody else? Boone? Don't you want to help your own father?"

"I will if Danny will," Boone says.

"Dsh," I say.

"You volunteers, you go help Mr. Barnaby for the rest of practice."

Babcock looks shocked. "You mean they won't have to run laps with us?" he asks.

"I guess not," Walt says.

"I'll help, too," Babcock says, pushing his glasses up on his nose.

"Too late," Walt says. "They've got enough already."

Mr. Barnaby says, "That's okay. I could use Babcock. For goalie training."

"Thank you, sir," Babcock says. And he wipes his face with the blue handkerchief that he always carries in his pocket.

Babcock *hates* running.

First thing, Mr. Barnaby tries to have us help with a kicking drill. All the Noodledoods stand in line and take turns trying to kick the ball into the goal — kick a ball that isn't even moving. Simplest thing in the world. No goalie, either.

The first kid runs up at the ball, swings a big kick with his right foot, misses the ball completely, and falls flat on his back. And lies there, laughing.

"That's terrible," I say.

"Very *good*, Timothy," Mr. Barnaby says. "You *almost* got it that time."

The next kid runs up and whacks the ball off the side of her toe. She misses the goal by a mile.

"No. Wrong," I say.

"Nice *shot*, Pamela," Mr. Barnaby says. "You got a good piece of it."

Next kid. This one is Clover. Boone's sister. Mr. Barnaby's daughter. She runs up to the ball and then can't decide which foot to use. She stops, then backs up and tries again. This time she doesn't stop, but she still doesn't know which foot to use and gets tangled up and trips over the ball and flies sprawling onto the grass.

"Oh, *Jesus*," I say.

"Nice try, Clover," Mr. Barnaby says.

By the time practice is over, I think I know exactly why the team lost fourteen to nothing.

After practice, Boone invites me to dinner at his house.

"You won't tell about Pop being gone. Right?" I say.

"I won't," Boone says.

They live under the trees at the edge of the red-wood forest. I take seconds on everything, even the green beans. And I say to Mr. Barnaby, "You got to get tougher on those kids. Those Noodledoods."

"Tougher? How?"

"Yell at 'em. Bawl 'em out. Tell 'em what they're doing wrong."

"I believe in positive coaching," Mr. Barnaby says.

"What's that?"

"You tell them what they're doing *right*. And praise them for it. They already know what they're doing wrong. They're *trying* to do it right. They just need encouragement. They *want* to do well. If you dump on them, they'll quit. I want them to feel good about themselves. They'll try harder if they feel good about it."

"But they *stink*!"

"We do not," Clover says with her mouth full of muffin. "We're Noodledoods. Noodledoods *never* stink."

"Danny, I want no more of that kind of talk," Mr. Barnaby says. "If you want to help with the team, you'll do it my way."

"Okay," I say.

"Good," Mr. Barnaby says, "because I need you. I have an announcement to make. I can't be at the game next Saturday. I need you guys to be in charge. You, Danny, and you, Boone, and Dylan and Geraldine and Babcock. Tell them to come to the game. You'll be the coaches."

"Really? That's *great*," Boone says.

I don't know if it's so great. Do I want to be in charge of those kids? They don't know a soccer ball from a giant mushroom. And I don't think I've got the hang of this positive coaching, yet. But I'll try. I need to stay on the good side of Mr. Barnaby, so I can come back for dinner sometimes.

"You know what?" Clover says.

"What?" Mr. Barnaby says.

"If you sleep with a book under your pillow, when you wake up you'll know what's in the book."

"Is that so?" Mr. Barnaby says.

"Yes, Daddy, and the only problem is if you drop the book the next day, you'll forget everything you learned. Unless you kiss the book before you pick it up."

"Kissing the book?" Mr. Barnaby says. "Is that like lip-reading?"

"No, Daddy."

"Well, Clover, I guess the brain works in mysterious ways."

I'm listening to Clover — I never knew you could learn a book by sleeping on it — but also when nobody is looking, I stuff two muffins under my shirt. Some of the crumbs fall into my pants. If I asked, they'd give them to me. But they'd start wondering what's going on at my house.

It ain't stealing if you take something they'd give you anyway.

Mr. Barnaby gives me a ride home in his Volkswagen bus. While he's driving, I say, thinking out loud, "I wonder what it's like."

"What?" Mr. Barnaby says.

"Being normal. I mean, having *normal* parents. Like you and Mrs. Barnaby."

Mr. Barnaby laughs. He says, "Nobody's normal. Especially in San Puerco. This is a town for cranks and dreamers."

"But *you're* normal."

"I'll try to forgive you for saying that."

I see he doesn't want to be called normal. It's true that there are a lot of oddballs in San Puerco, probably more than most places. Most folk in San Puerco don't have enough money to live in the suburbs, and wouldn't like it even if they could. But Mr. Barnaby's a lot more normal than my father.

Nothing but a four-wheel drive could handle my driveway, so Mr. Barnaby lets me off at the side of the road. Jogging down to the trailer, I check to see just in case Pop came home. But no lights are on.

I didn't really expect him. But I sort of hoped.

I'll admit it: Sometimes he ain't the greatest father. Only once did he come to one of my soccer games ever in my life, and I hope he never does again because all he did was yell at the ref. He hates refs. Or cops. Or schoolteachers. Or anybody who can tell somebody else what to do. He's strange that way. He flies off the handle. I have to calm him down, and usually I can, just by saying his name. "Hey, Pop, relax," I say. And he snaps out of it.

But I couldn't talk him out of the tree.

Other times, though, like the night we played poker or the night we went to the graveyard, I wouldn't trade him for anybody. But what's the point of wondering? You don't choose your old man. He's the only father I've got. He's street. And at least when he's home, there's usually food in the fridge.

I take the muffins out from under my shirt. I leave one outside the coyote hole, hoping they'll get the idea I ain't trying to poison them. I kick off my shoes and sit on the bed and see the grammar book I left on my pillow. I was supposed to review a chapter for school. I'm tired. I open the book to the right chapter and set it under my pillow. Then I lay down with my head on the pillow. That way, when I wake up tomorrow, I'll know my lesson.

I lie with my eyes open. I can almost feel the words slipping into my head from the book under the pillow. The moon is coming up. I'm just lying in a trailer in the middle of nowhere, surrounded by cows. It's lonelier this night, after eating at Boone's. And I don't want to fall asleep, don't want to dream. Dreams aren't fun for me. Not when they're bad.

I hear scuffling.

I look down from the window, and there go the two coyotes up the driveway.

I break into a grin, which I thought was totally silent, but the coyotes stop and look back at me. Their eyes catch the moonlight like little balls of fire. Wildfire. Then they turn and keep on going up the driveway. In a moment I'm up and out of the trailer, tying my shoes and following as quietly as I can.

They look back once again. I'm a hundred feet away. I freeze. Pop says if you hold absolutely still, a coyote can't see you. With those big ears, though, I bet they can hear me breathing, and with those noses, even from a hundred feet away I probably smell like a three-day-old sock. But then, they don't smell so good to me, either. Even with my weak little human nose I can tell they've been rolling in some dead carcass full of maggots. They wear it like perfume.

They don't seem to mind that I'm following. They don't run away. They just keep on going. I feel like they invited me. I keep on following to the edge of the farmyard — where I stop.

The farmyard is an open space with a farmhouse on one side, a barn on another, a toolshed, a pile of rusty old machinery, and a chicken coop.

Sleeping under the porch in front of the farmhouse I see Goldie, the farmer's dog. I can see just half of her curled up with her nose tucked under her tail. Goldie's this old stiff-leg collie who never was too bright to begin with, and now she's lost her hearing and half her eyesight. Goldie just lies under the porch all day and all night. It takes something powerful, like a cherry bomb, to wake her, and then she runs out and barks and tries to bite something — anything — the first thing she runs into, which might be a person or a sapling tree or the fender of the farmer's pickup truck. The farmer's name is Hoggle, Henry Hoggle. He must be sleeping. All the lights are off in the house.

One coyote, the male, stands by the toolshed. The female slinks across the open space to the chicken coop. She sniffs around. Then she looks to the male and sort of nods her head.

The male trots over. He sniffs around at the chicken wire.

The night is quiet — but not silent. It's an alive quiet, with rustlings of wind and crickets and owls.

The two coyotes start pawing and nuzzling and testing the chicken wire. In a few minutes, being coyotes which means being smart, they figure it out. Working together they dig an opening under the chicken wire.

The female scoots under the fence and into the coop.

A second later, it's like a bomb went off. Squawk! Squawk! Screech! Squawk! Goldie wakes up and starts woofing. In the coop there's a thump and a crash and more squawking and screeching — and the screen door slams at the farmhouse. Here comes Hoggle in white pajamas. With a rifle. Goldie runs out and bites the first thing she runs into — which is Hoggle. On the leg. He tries to kick her off.

The male coyote runs for the shed.

Blam! Hoggle shoots.

The coyote jumps. Was he hit? He's gone. Out of sight. Vanished.

The female scoots out from under the fence and tears toward the barn with a chicken in her mouth. Hoggle takes aim. Goldie runs between his legs.

Blam!

The she coyote jerks to the side. She leaps, and she's gone. Was she hit?

Hoggle runs toward where he last saw her. He

pokes around outside the barn. Goldie runs around in circles, woofing like a maniac.

Hoggle gives up and grabs Goldie by the collar and hauls her back to the porch.

They got away. But are they wounded? And will they ever come back? Will I see them again?

Hoggle goes into the house. Goldie crawls under the porch.

Again, the night is quiet. But not the same quiet as before. A quiet like being dead.

I don't want to be alone in my trailer.

Keeping out of Hoggle's sight, I walk out to the road, then climb the fence and wander up to the graveyard at the top of the hill. The moon covers everything with a silver light. I can see Hoggle's house, the chicken coop, barn, shed. Down below I see my trailer with a silver gleam. The cattle are all sleeping. Away in a pasture that I can just barely see, a rancher keeps sheep who look like balls of dandelion fluff in the grass. Everything's peaceful and quiet, except I'm worried somewhere there's a couple coyotes bleeding to death.

An airplane winks across the sky. First it's silent, then the sound comes after the jet has already passed. Then the sky is quiet again, and I can hear the soft murmuring of the grass in the wind. My body casts a shadow. A moonshadow.

Then I hear it. *Yap-yap ow-oooo! Ow-ooo!* From not too far. And right away, there's an answer from the other side of the hill: *Yap-yap ow-oooo!*

I see them. They must've split up when Hoggle fired at them, then they howled to find each other, and now I see them loping toward one another on the side of the hill.

Look at them! Two coyotes in the moonlight. Savvy — that's what they are. Savvy. Wild. Daring. Totally *street*. The most beautiful sight I think I've ever seen. They belong on this land. They're as natural as grass.

When they meet, it looks like they kiss. They go, "Yip," and they sort of nip each other on the muzzle — soft, with a little whiny sound. Then they set off at a trot down the hill together with their big bushy tails shimmering in the silver light.

6
BUSINESS

I'm in the group shower where the walls are white
tile and the air is steam, and here comes Big Al,
Big ugly Al, the big white body half muscle and half
fat and none of it brain, a belly button that sticks
out like a bottle cap, and I wonder if I pop that cap
off if the guts would foam out like he'd been shook
before he was opened, and he says I got to make
his bed for him because I didn't give him my dessert
last night, and I say I ain't making his bed or giving
him my dessert, and the next thing I know, his fist
is cracking my nose. I slip on the wet floor. He's
on me with his hands on my neck so I can't suck
air, and I hear his breath in my ear and a pain that
I don't recognize, and I kick out with my feet and
roll away, and there's blood in the water on the
floor, my blood washing down the drain, and I touch

my ear and the fingers come away red, and there's blood dripping onto my shoulder and running across my chest in a little stream down my leg, and I shout

"Whoa!"

and jerk up in my bed. Morning. The same dream. I'm in a sweat. Out of breath. In my own bed, in a room the size of a closet, in a trailer on a farm. Alone.

For breakfast I eat one of the muffins I took from Boone's house. The other is lying on the ground outside, crawling with bugs. The coyotes didn't touch it. They're too wild. Too stubborn. Too scared of poison. I'm still hungry, so I drink two glasses of water. But water doesn't fool my stomach into thinking it's full. It wants more food.

I set off walking to school up the driveway, which is just two tracks of dirt.

At the top of the driveway I meet Hoggle. He's built like a brick chimney, kind of square and red and getting bigger at the bottom. Smokes, too.

"Mornin', Danny," he says. "Want an apple?" It's in his hand. In his other hand he has a basket, which he uses for collecting eggs.

I look at that red apple, streaked with yellow and green, thinking: Should I eat it now for breakfast, or save it for dinner?

"I'll take it. Thanks." And I put it to my teeth. So much for wondering if I should save it. My body made the choice without even asking my brain for advice.

"Lost a chicken," Hoggle says.

"Dsh," I say. Of course I know who got that chicken.

"Come over here and take a look at this chicken coop," he says. "See that hole? I had to come out here last night and shoot at a couple coyotes. Think I got one."

I know he missed, but I don't say.

Hoggle scowls at Goldie.

"Varmints," Hoggle says. "Thought we'd killed them all. Now they're back. Will you tell your daddy to fix the coop?"

Part of the agreement we have with Hoggle is that my father is supposed to do some work around the place in exchange for the low rent. Only, Pop never does anything.

"He's busy today," I say.

"Busy!" Hoggle throws up his hands. "He made a deal. He's supposed to help. Because of the low rent."

"He says the rent ain't all that low."

"A deal's a deal. What about you? Will you fix it?"

"I didn't make no deal."

"Your daddy did. And you're part of it."

"I never made no deal. Why don't you fix it yourself, Mr. Hoggle?"

"Hurts my back. Hurts it *bad*. Want some advice? Don't ever get old, Danny. That's my advice. Don't ever get old."

"I don't plan to."

Actually, Pop says Hoggle only talks old when the subject is farming.

"Good plan. Tell you what. I'll pay you to fix the coop. How's that? You could earn some money."

"How much?"

"Two dollars."

"Total? Or two dollars an hour?"

"All right. Two dollars an hour."

"I'll have to do more than just fill the hole," I say. "They'll just dig a new one. We got to make it so he can't dig under."

"You do it. One thing I know about you, Danny — you're inventive. You can figure out something. There's wire in the shed. Shovel. Look around for anything else you need. Oughta be in there. You can do it. Probably do it better than that no-account father of yours."

"Dsh!"

"What?"

"He ain't no-account. He's my *father*."

"Hey. Sorry."

"You can fix your own chicken coop, Mr. Hoggle. I ain't — "

"Hey. Cool down. I said I'm sorry. Look. I need your help. How about this? I'll pay you *three* dollars an hour."

Hm. I didn't mean to turn down the job. I needed it. When I get mad, though, sometimes I say things I later regret. The moment I told Hoggle to fix his own chicken coop, I felt sorry — but I couldn't help it. Now Hoggle was giving me a second chance — and an extra dollar an hour. Maybe it's good luck, burying an Elvis.

"Okay," I say. "It's a deal."

"Good. That, and a new dog, and we'll stop them varmints."

"You getting a new dog, Mr. Hoggle?"

"Yep, Danny, I think it's time. Poor old Goldie. She's no help."

A car pulls off the road into the farmyard. A BMW. A man gets out and greets Hoggle. Goldie doesn't even wake up, which is a good thing because if she did, she'd probably run out and bite something — the man, or his car.

I wish I could open the hood and look at the engine of the BMW. I like motors.

"I see you finished the tractor work," the man says. He wears a suit and tie. "I came to pay you."

Hoggle hires himself out to do tractor work now and then. He has a beat-up old backhoe and dozer. And Pop says Hoggle never complains about being too old for backhoe work. Not when there's good money to be made.

"Roots," Hoggle says.

"What?" the man asks.

"I'm afraid I ran into some problems," Hoggle

says. "Roots. Took longer than I expected. Lot of roots."

The man frowns. He looks at his watch. He says, "How much do I owe you?"

"It came to eight hours," Hoggle says. "At sixty-five dollars an hour."

"I thought you said sixty."

"Did I? Well, well. I forgot. You get a bargain, then. Sixty."

The man writes a check.

Something tells me that man will never hire Hoggle again. Nobody does, hardly, anymore.

With the man gone, Hoggle notices me again. "You still here?" he says. "What're you staring at?"

I didn't know I was staring. Since he asked, I say, "I saw you leave for that job last Saturday. And I heard you come back. About lunchtime. You were gone for four hours."

"So?"

"You told him eight."

"So?"

"So that's what I was staring at."

"Staring at my business?"

"I call it something else."

Hoggle frowns. "No, no. That's business." He scratches his neck. "Danny, if you're going to make a living in this world, you better understand business. Like your daddy. Look at all the work he does around here."

"He don't work around here."

"Exactly. He understands business a little too well. Now maybe you should start learning. First of all, you need to learn when to hold your mouth."

"You asked. You asked what I was staring at. That's why I said — "

"You don't go talking to that man who paid me."

"I won't."

"Second of all, you got to learn how to price yourself. How much to charge."

"How much, Mr. Hoggle?"

"All that the market will bear."

"What if that man comes back later and says you charged too much?"

"It's a done deal. No givebacks. Never no givebacks, Danny."

"Okay."

"And it helps to have a motto. For your business."

"What's yours, Mr. Hoggle?"

"Eat the rich." He laughs.

"That's a motto?"

He's still smiling. I can see he's enjoying himself. "And most important of all," he says, "you got to have the right business philosophy."

"The what?"

"Philosophy. The way you do business. Your way of seeing things."

"What's yours, Mr. Hoggle?"

"Mine? *Screw everybody*." He laughs again and

shakes all over. When he finally calms down, he says, "Now excuse me, Danny. I got to collect the morning eggs."

"Mr. Hoggle!"

"What?"

"Can I collect the eggs for you?"

"You bet. I'd be glad. You know where to look?"

"I think so."

In the coop I find nine eggs. I put seven in the basket and two in my shirt. It ain't stealing. It's business. Hoggle said so himself.

On the way to school, I stop and suck the eggs. Raw. I shouldn't be this hungry, I tell myself. I had a big dinner last night at Boone's. And a muffin and an apple this morning. But somehow, not knowing where supper is coming from, I just want to stuff myself. Because I might not be able to, later.

I walk to school.

Walking's too slow. I could build a bike out of scrap pieces. Besides the two wheels, I have some other parts I found some time ago: a handlebar, a seat, and a chain. I just need a frame and some pedals. Then some day I can ride, instead of walk.

Some day when business is better.

At school it seemed that I knew the grammar from sleeping on the book. At least, it sounded familiar when Mrs. Rule explained it.

For lunch on Tuesdays they always serve

chipped beef on toast. It looks — and smells — like vomit on a plate.

Boone opens his lunch bag and says, "I brought an extra sandwich for you. You want it, Danny?"

Before I can answer, Babcock grabs it. "Can I have it?" he says. He's already finished his thermos of powder and water.

He's even hungrier than I am. I take a forkful of chipped beef. "You can have it," I say.

"Thanks, Danny. Thanks, Boone." And Babcock wolfs it down.

Boone watches the sandwich disappear. "I figured you could save it for dinner," he says to me.

"It's all right," I say. "Babcock needs it, too. Anyway, I can come to your house for dinner."

"Not tonight," Boone says. "We've got company."

"I'd invite you to my house for dinner," Babcock says, "but all we're having is you-know-what."

His you-know-what makes even chipped beef look good.

"Don't worry about me," I say. "I'll take care of myself."

After school I was walking home along Creek Road on the part after Disappearing Creek has disappeared when I walked right into a spider web. A big one. It stuck to my face and hair. I had to stop and pick it off — careful, of course, so I wouldn't kill the spider if he happened to be on me. If you kill a spider, you know, you'll be poor for the rest of your life. If you believe that stuff. Which I don't. But I still didn't want to kill the spider, just in case. Like Pop would say, the best ain't worth the worst.

The other thing about spiders is that if you walk into one of their webs, it means you'll meet a friend. But I ain't superstitious like Pop.

I was still picking sticky strands of webbing off my chin when a white Jaguar passed me, then stopped in the middle of the road. It purred like a pussycat. I wanted to throw open that long sleek hood and look around inside. You don't see Jaguars in San Puerco. I stared. Then it backed up. The driver, a woman with blonde hair, lowered her window with an electric humming sound. "Excuse me, young man," she said.

"Who, me?" I said. I wondered if I was in trouble for staring at her car.

"Do you live here?"

"Near."

"Oh, *excellent*. We're new here, and I don't know where to *find* anything."

"*You* live here?"

"Right there," she said, and she pointed to a driveway about a hundred feet up the road.

I'd seen construction trucks going in and out of that driveway for the last year, and I'd figured somebody was building a house, but I'd never seen it. The driveway winds into some trees and goes out of sight.

"Do you know where I can hire a carpenter?" she asked.

I said, "What about the carpenters who built your house?"

"Oh, they're long gone," she said. "The house is *finished*."

"Then why do you need a carpenter?"

"Well, you see, we just bought a Ping-Pong table for Law. This is Law," she said, turning toward the back seat.

I hadn't been able to see anybody in the back seat because the windows were tinted dark. Now I leaned forward and peered in through the woman's open window, and sure enough there was a boy back there. He looked near my age. Blond with blue eyes. A clean shirt. Combed hair.

"My name's Laurence," he said. "They call me Law."

"Hi, Law," I said. "My name's Danny."

"Oh, *excellent*," the woman said. "It's so hard for Law to meet people when he doesn't go to the school."

"How does he get out of going to school?"

"He goes to the Academy."

I'd heard of the Academy. It's a private school for rich kids over the hill.

"Anyway," the woman said, "we wanted Law to get more exercise, so we bought him a Ping-Pong table. But it came in a box. We need a carpenter to assemble it."

"A carpenter? I bet all you need is a screwdriver and a wrench."

"Yes. Somebody with tools."

"Don't you have a screwdriver?"

"Of course not."

"Jeez, lady, even *I* could do that."

"Would you?"

"You mean, me?"

"Didn't you just say you could?"

"Yes."

"Oh, *excellent*. You can assemble it, and then you and Law can play Ping-Pong. He needs to make some friends. And he needs the exercise. Why don't you come and stay for dinner? Wouldn't that be *excellent*? Then we could get to *know* you."

"That would be — um — excellent," I said. Food. Dinner. Definitely excellent. "But I have some work I promised to do after school today."

"Could you come later?"

"Yes, ma'am, I'd be glad to."

"My name is Mrs. Livermore."

"Yes, Mrs. Livermore."

"And bring your tools."

"Yes, ma'am."

All this time Law hadn't said a word since telling me his name. Now he spoke: "Do you have any baseball cards?"

"Some," I said.

"Bring 'em," he said.

The car drove away, and for the first time I noticed the license plate:

XLNT

I wondered how she'd earned the money for a car that cost more than my father had earned in my entire lifetime. It occurred to me that Mrs. Livermore had been willing to hire a carpenter, and now I was going to do the job for free.

That wasn't good business. I needed to learn business — learn it *fast* — if I wanted to survive 'til Pop came back.

7
WHITEKNIGHT

I come to fix the chicken coop and find Hoggle with his head buried in the engine of his pickup truck, and a great white shark sitting on the ground next to Hoggle's boots. That is, it has the teeth and the big cruel eyes of a shark, but it has white fur and four legs. When it sees me, it leaps toward me and growls at my pocket.

I stop dead.

Hoggle lifts his head out from under the hood. "Hey! Whiteknight! It's all right."

Whiteknight, the shark, stands there growling. I hold out my hand. Whiteknight sniffs. His fur is erect. His paws are gigantic.

Hoggle calls, "Whiteknight! Back off!"

The shark doesn't budge.

Hoggle smiles and says, "How do you like my new

dog? Looks like he takes his job pretty serious."

I start talking to the shark: "Easy, there, big boy. Easy, Whiteknight." I hold out my hand again. I keep saying, "Easy, boy. Take it easy. You can sniff my hand just as long as you want. Easy, now."

The tip of his tail gives the tiniest wag.

Hoggle leans back under the hood.

It takes me five minutes to sweet talk Whiteknight into letting me pass. All this time, Goldie is sound asleep under the porch. Finally I get by, and I walk up to the truck. It's a beat-up old GMC pickup. Once I asked Hoggle what GMC stood for, and he said, "General Mess of Crap."

I peek over the fender and say, "Whatcha doing, Mr. Hoggle?"

He pulls his head, then his arms, then his hands, out from under the hood. They're covered all over with black grease, even his face, which is usually red. He puts a hand on his back.

"Quitting," he says.

"Is it broke?"

"Naw. I just wanted to change the oil. But I can't get the filter off. And my back hurts. I'm gonna go lie down. I'll have to take it to a garage. Those bandits will charge me twenty bucks to do this. Don't ever get old, Danny."

"You can't take it to the garage."

"Why not?"

"Because you already drained the oil." I could see the pan under the truck.

"Hmm. You're right." He scratches his head, smearing grease in his hair. "Tomorrow, maybe, my back will feel better."

"Can I try? I know how. I've watched you before."

Hoggle looks at me, and suddenly his face softens into a look of kindness. He says, "I bet you do know how. And I bet you wish your father had a car."

"That's true. I do."

"Be my guest. There's the new filter. Five quarts of oil. Socket wrench. Toolbox."

"Okay. You lie down."

"Gladly." He walks away, bent forward.

"Hey."

"What?"

"Will you pay me for this?"

Hoggle stops walking, still bent over. He presses a hand against his back just above his big old butt. "Not twenty bucks, I won't."

"Ten?"

"Five."

"Seven-fifty?"

"Six."

"Deal," I say, and Hoggle shuffles off to his house.

Good deal, I'm thinking. Just call me Danny Business.

I stand on the bumper so I can reach inside the engine. Hoggle left the filter wrench hanging on the filter. I can see why he couldn't get it off: He was turning it the wrong way. He was *tightening* it. His back must be hurting bad, or he would've figured it out. People get dumber when they hurt. Pop gets headaches, and he'll walk into walls. I take the wrench off and put it back on the other way. I push.

It won't budge. He's tightened it too much.

I put both hands on the wrench and brace my body against the radiator. Push.

Won't budge.

I pull out the drain pan, then crawl under the engine, reach up with both hands, and hang with all my weight on the wrench.

Won't budge.

Still hanging, I pull my body up with my elbows and then drop, bouncing so all the weight goes to my hands.

It moves. Just a bit.

I bounce again. It moves some more. Now I can turn it. It screws off, with me lying under it, and as it comes off it falls right on my forehead with a clunk that hurts, and I say "Ow!" and warm black oil dribbles over my nose and into my mouth.

But at least I got it off.

I crawl out from under the truck, spit out the oil, and wipe my face with my sleeve.

The taste of oil reminds my belly how hungry it is. It likes a snack after school. And I think it's worried about whether I'll get any dinner at all. I can tell my brain not to worry, I'll get dinner at the Livermores' or else I'll figure out something, and my brain will believe. I could even tell myself I already ate. If I have to, I can fool my brain. But not my belly. It starts churning. Howling. It's so hungry, it wants to eat motor oil!

I screw the new filter onto the motor. Then I open a can of oil and pour it into the hole. And another. And another. Five cans.

Something is oozy under my shoes. I look down. Fresh oil. Coming from under the truck. I get down on my knees.

Oops.

I forgot to put the drain plug back in. All the new oil drained out the bottom as fast as I was pouring it into the top.

I lie down with my back in the pool of oil and screw in the drain plug and tighten it with the socket wrench.

Now what? I already used up all the oil. Got to do something. I search the toolshed. Then the barn. No oil. My shirt that laid in the oil is sticking to my back.

Whiteknight watches me suspiciously. Goldie sleeps.

Street situation. Got to buy oil. All I have is a nickel.

I knock on the door to the farmhouse. Mrs. Hoggle answers, "Yes, Danny?"

"Could I talk to Mr. Hoggle?"

"He's resting right now. Could I help?"

"He said he'd pay me. To change the oil in his truck."

"Well, I can pay you," she says, and she fetches her purse. "How much?"

"Um. Eight dollars."

Why not? It was Hoggle who taught me.

I run to the store. Oil costs a dollar thirty-nine a can, plus tax. I buy five cans, one Hershey bar, and a red-hot. Eight dollars and three cents. I walk back eating the Hershey bar, then sucking the red-hot. Gets that oil taste out of my mouth. Also, it makes my stomach stop hollering, at least for a while.

Whiteknight lets me into the farmyard. But I can see he doesn't like it.

And I don't like this dog.

I pour the oil into the filler hole. This time, it stays. I screw on the cap, shut the hood.

Guess I still got some things to learn about business.

Almost dinnertime. No time to fix the chicken coop. There's a pile of boards in the barn. I haul a couple over to the coop and cover the hole where the coyotes got in. Something's under one board, holding it up off the ground so it can't lie flat. A brick. I pull out the brick and toss it toward the house.

Oops.

The brick hits the dirt in front of the porch, bounces up and lands on Goldie's rear.

The old collie springs up. She comes out woofing.

She's searching with her half-blind eyes for something to bite.

Whiteknight's running right behind her. He's barking, too. He doesn't know what all the commotion is about, but whatever it is, he wants to be part of it.

Goldie with her stiff legs runs woofing in a half circle and crashes into a wheelbarrow. The wheelbarrow falls on its side with Goldie on top of it and then rolls over on its back. Goldie gives a yelp, twists her head, and sinks her teeth into the wheelbarrow's tire. There's a sound like sort of a halfhearted pop, like there wasn't too much pressure in the tire to begin with, and then a long wheeze.

Whiteknight sizes up the action, lunges for the tire with a vicious slashing bite, and then, snarling, starts tearing the tire to bits. Goldie's satisfied with her one bite. The upside-down wheelbarrow, with its legs in the air, probably looks to her cloudy eyes like a dog saying, "I quit. You win."

The screen door opens, and Hoggle steps out. He sees Goldie curling herself up by the porch. He sees Whiteknight demolishing the wheelbarrow. Whiteknight has totally vaporized the tire and is now chomping and tearing at the wooden legs.

Whiteknight reminds me of Big Al at The Miracle Home. He'd never let up, either.

Hoggle shakes his head, presses his hand against his back, and goes inside.

I pity any animal who gets in Whiteknight's way.

8
IN PURSUIT
OF EXCELLENCE

With the sun going down, I ran along Creek Road and into the driveway to the Livermores' house. It was gigantic. Just the garage could've held three trailers the size of the one I was living in. There were bay windows and arched windows and stained-glass windows and sliding-door windows — and the most complicated roof I'd ever seen. It looked like each room had its own different height with its own different roof, like a whole city skyline all joined together somehow. I wondered how they would keep it from leaking. My trailer had the simplest roof in the world, and it leaked.

The front door had a big brass doorknocker and a doorbell. First I rang the bell, then I tapped the knocker.

Mrs. Livermore opened the door. She was wearing a white dress. She held a cocktail glass in her hand. "My God," she said.

"Hello," I said. "Remember me?"

"I remember somebody who looked like you," she said. "But he was *clean*."

"I told you I had some work to do."

"What happened to your clothes? Your face? You didn't say you were going to work in a *coal mine*."

"It's just oil," I said. "Oil and dirt."

"Did you have to *wallow* in it?"

"I guess I had to lie down."

"Oh *dear*. I'm sorry. But you can't come in."

Just then Law came to the door and stood beside his mother. "Did you bring your baseball cards?" he asked.

I held up a small greasy paper bag. "Right here," I said. "And a couple of screwdrivers and a wrench."

"Not tonight, Law," Mrs. Livermore said. "Some other time."

"I'll loan him some clothes," Law said.

"He needs a *bath*."

"Fine," Law said. "We've got a bathroom. We've got *four* bathrooms."

"Oh no. Not in this house. He'll get the tub dirty."

That sounded like a dsh situation to me. You get in a bathtub to get clean. But they won't let you in because you'll get the tub dirty.

"Then I'll clean him outside," Law said.

"How?"

"With water. Wait there, Danny."

Mrs. Livermore sighed, raised her eyes to the ceiling, and took a sip from her cocktail glass.

Law returned with clothes, a towel, a bar of soap, and a scrub brush. "Follow me," he said. He led me to the side of the house where there was a hose neatly rolled up on a reel.

"You got warm water in that hose?" I asked.

"Sorry," Law said.

I noticed a banana slug, bright yellow, eight inches long, ugly, slimy, oozy, with a red spot on its back, sliding slowly between my feet. I'd never seen one with a red spot before.

The sun was down, but some light was still lingering in the sky. A cool wind was blowing. I said, "Now what?"

"Strip."

I took off my clothes. Suddenly the wind seemed stronger. And colder. Then Law turned on the hose.

"AAAGH!"

I jumped. I shivered. I hopped. I came down on the banana slug and squashed it with my foot.

"Here," Law said, shutting off the hose. He tossed me a bar of soap.

I washed as fast as I could. I was breathing in short little bursts. Shaking. Goose bumps all over.

"You'll have to scrub," Law said, and he tossed me the brush.

The bristles scraped me like knives. The oil came out, but so did a layer of skin. I was raw. The hardest part to wash wasn't the oil or the dirt but the slug on the bottom of my foot — they stick like chewing gum.

"Now rinse," Law said, and he turned on the hose again.

"AAA-AAAGH!"

The cold water on my raw skin felt like fire — like I was burning. Like when you touch the wet skin under a popped blister.

"Now dry," Law said, tossing me a towel.

I never dressed so fast in my life. His clothes fit okay. We were the same height, but I was thinner. Nice clothes: no holes. Not even frayed. Thick cotton.

"Now can we eat?" I said, jumping up and down with my arms folded across my chest, trying to get warm.

"It won't be ready yet. My stepfather comes home late. We don't usually eat for another hour."

If I'd known what I was getting into when I agreed to go there that night, I might've decided that the best, being dinner, wasn't worth the worst, being the hose. But I wasn't going to quit now.

"What's it like?" Law asked.

"What's what like?"

"Being so dirty. Is it fun?"

I shrugged. "I dunno. Maybe."

"Let's see your baseball cards," Law said.

I opened the paper bag.

"That's all?" he said.

"I ain't a collector."

"Why not?"

"I just ain't." I didn't want to say that I don't ever have any money so I can't buy any cards. Most of my collection came from Boone. He gave me his duplicates. Plus I got some from chewing gum, sometimes, when Pop had extra change in his pocket.

"Do you have a big collection?" I asked.

"Eighteen thousand, four hundred cards," Law said.

"Do you know if the Giants beat the Reds today?"

"No. How would I know?"

"It was on the radio."

"I don't listen to baseball games on the radio."

"You watch them on television?"

"No. It's too boring."

"You *go* to baseball games?"

"No."

"You *play* baseball?"

"No."

Another dsh situation, if you ask me. But maybe I could make some money out of it. I said, "You want to buy my cards?"

"I might. You know how much they're worth?"

I figured the stack of cards, if I bought them as packs of bubble gum in the store, would cost about ten dollars. But these weren't new anymore. Some of the players weren't even playing anymore. So I said, "Five dollars, maybe."

I expected him to laugh, or at least to make a

lower offer, but Law just said, "Okay." He reached into his pocket, pulled out a folded wad of bills, and peeled off five ones.

I looked at that green paper in his hand. Most of my friends don't carry any money around with them, much less a wad of bills.

"What are you staring at?" Law asked. "Changing your mind?"

"No," I said, and I took the money before he could change his.

"I guess you should take a look at that Ping-Pong table. There's probably still time before dinner."

Law showed me to the garage, which was big enough for three cars, though only one, the **XLNT** white Jaguar, was parked there at the time. We pulled the table out of the box. All I had to do was bolt the legs onto the tabletop. It took about five minutes.

"You want to play a game?" I asked.

He shrugged. "I'm supposed to," he said.

"You know how?"

"No."

So I taught him. He caught on fast. I could beat him, of course, but to keep it interesting, I let him come close.

Mrs. Livermore came into the garage and clapped her hands and said, "Oh isn't this *excellent*?" She smiled happily. "Now don't overdo it on the first day, Law. You know you need to work into these things *gradually*."

Law ignored her and served the ball. He'd discovered I wasn't as good when I had to hit backhand, so he was aiming all his volleys to that side.

Suddenly the garage door opened, and a gleaming green Jaguar drove in and parked next to the white one. A man got out, nodded curtly at Law, and went into the house. Law ignored him. The license plate on the green Jag said

I ERND IT

Law was quick with his hands, which is basically what Ping-Pong is all about. I made the mistake of putting a spin on a few of the balls I hit, and Law saw what I was doing and started putting a spin on his returns, only better. The ball was hopping all over the table, taking crazy bounces.

"Dinnertime," Mrs. Livermore called.

Just in time. I was getting a headache trying to keep up with his spinners.

"Take off your shoes before you go in the house," Law said to me.

When I stepped inside, I saw why. The carpet was white — even in the dining room. The furniture wasn't modern; in fact, it looked old — antiques, I guess — but everything was polished to a high shine. There was a chandelier over the dining room table that must've had three hundred crystals, each one sparkling. Mrs. Livermore with her blonde hair and diamond earrings looked just as sparkling.

"You sure keep a clean house," I said as I sat down.

"Thank you," Mrs. Livermore said.

"I found some dirt in the closet this morning," Mr. Livermore said. "Under my shoes."

"I'm sorry," Mrs. Livermore said.

"You have to watch those housecleaners," Mr. Livermore said. "That's your job."

"Yes. I'm sorry. It won't happen again."

Mr. Livermore looked like one of those television newscasters with the blow-dried hair and the aviator glasses, except he was older than those guys. In fact, he looked a lot older than Mrs. Livermore. His shoulders curved forward. His mouth looked tight. He could smile if he needed to, but I don't think he could've really *grinned* — not without breaking his jaw.

"It's a lot of hard work," Mr. Livermore said, "but I think it's worth the sacrifice. I think a clean house is a sign of self-respect. Don't you, young man?"

"Yes, sir," I said. "I suppose it is."

"That's why we have the housecleaners come every day of the week. Not just once a week like *some* people."

"Yes, sir."

"Oh, excuse us, Danny," Mrs. Livermore said, placing a hand on my arm and glancing at her husband. "He didn't mean to imply — oh, dear, I hope we weren't *insensitive* — I mean, if your family only cleans once a week, he didn't mean to say —

do you have a housecleaner come once a week?"

"No, ma'am."

"Ah. *Excellent.* Then you must know what we mean."

"Yes, ma'am."

"We have declared *war* on dirt."

I thought: If they saw my trailer, they just might have to surrender. I also had the feeling that when she said "we," she meant "he."

"Speaking of dirt," Mrs. Livermore said, turning to her husband, "now that the house is finished, it's time to do something about the yard."

"Fine," Mr. Livermore said. "Hire a landscaper."

"It's not that simple," Mrs. Livermore said. "There are slugs out there."

"Fine," Mr. Livermore said. "Hire an exterminator."

"I saw a slug," I said. "Out by your hose."

Mr. Livermore scowled at me. "Did you kill it?" he said.

"Yes," I said.

"Good."

"Ugh," Mrs. Livermore said. "Don't talk about it."

"We'll kill them all," Mr. Livermore said.

"Why?" I said.

"Because we don't like them," he said.

Something about the way he said that made me want to disagree with him. I've never been a fan of slugs. But I didn't like the idea of Mr. Livermore sitting in a chair on a white carpet in a totally dirtless house giving orders to wipe out a bunch of living creatures — disgusting, but living.

"Slugs don't hurt nobody," I said.

"Anybody," Mr. Livermore said.

"What?"

"*Anybody*," Mr. Livermore said. "Slugs don't hurt *anybody*."

"I'm glad you agree, sir."

Mr. Livermore slammed his hand on the table. "Hire an exterminator," he said, looking straight at me as if I was one more slug.

Law was hiding a smile behind his napkin.

"I have a better idea," Mrs. Livermore said. "One that will get rid of the slugs *and* the dirty dirt outside. We can put in a swimming pool. And a big concrete patio all around. Wouldn't that be *excellent*? And Law could even *swim* in it. He could get *exercise*. Won't it be nice to have pool parties? We could build an outdoor bar. And a barbecue. Like those wonderful pictures in *Sunset* magazine." She looked at her husband. "Wouldn't that be *excellent*, Nathan?"

"Fine," Mr. Livermore said, snapping his teeth onto a forkful of broccoli.

"Wouldn't that be good exercise, Law?" Mrs. Livermore asked.

Law's eyes looked glazed.

"Answer your mother," Mr. Livermore said.

"Yes, sir," Law said.

"Call me Father," Mr. Livermore said.

"Yes, Father," Law said. "Mother — it would be all right."

"Swimming is so *clean*," Mrs. Livermore said.

"If you want exercise," I said, "you should join our soccer team. We're short one player. We really need you. You ever play soccer, Law?"

"No."

"If your feet are as quick as your hands, you'll be good."

"Really?" Law looked pleased with the idea.

Mrs. Livermore looked worried. "Isn't that a rather *rough* game?" she asked, glancing nervously at her husband.

"It's refereed," I said. "We play clean."

"Do you play outdoors?"

"Of course."

"And don't you get sweaty? And dusty?"

"Well . . . yeah . . ."

"Then I'd hardly call that playing *clean*."

"I can take a shower afterwards, Mother," Law said.

"You'll have to buy some cleats," I said.

"No problem," Law said.

No problem. I hadn't gotten new cleats for two years. My feet had grown three sizes. But Pop said I had to squeeze one more year out of them.

Mrs. Livermore said, "Don't you think you're plunging into something a little too . . . *strenuous*?"

"I won't get carried away," Law promised.

"I suppose you could try it once," Mrs. Livermore

said. "But I think we still need a pool. Oh! I have a local resource right here at my table. That's you, Danny. Do you know where I can find somebody to dig a pool?"

"Henry Hoggle," I said. "He does tractor work."

Mr. Livermore leaned forward and looked me in the eye. "Is he good?" he asked.

I squirmed. I didn't want to lie and say he was good. But I didn't want to bad-mouth anybody, either. I remembered Hoggle's motto and his business philosophy. This would be the job he always dreamed of.

"Well," I said, "one thing's for sure. Hoggle knows his business."

Mr. Livermore leaned back in his chair. He'd finished eating. He poured himself another glass of liquor. "That's what I want," he said. "A man who knows what he's doing."

"He knows exactly what he's doing," I said.

9
GRAMMAR

After dinner I told Law I needed to change back into my own clothes so I could go home.

"Wear mine," Law said.

"Okay. I'll bring 'em back tomorrow."

"Keep them."

I ran toward home. I held my own oily clothes tucked under my arm.

In the center of San Puerco is a lake. In the daytime, kids play along the shoreline. People feed the ducks and try to dodge the mean old goose. Babcock comes down here to talk to dragonflies. At night, a different kind of people shows up. People with nothing better to do than sit in a pickup truck drinking beer and playing loud music with the windows rolled down so everybody else has to listen, too.

This night, though, there were no pickups. Just an old Volkswagen Beetle, which at first I thought was an abandoned car. But then I saw the glow of a cigarette inside.

As I was running by, an empty beer can came flying out the window from the Volkswagen and went rolling across the street. And a voice said, "Hey you! Come here!"

I stopped running. I looked toward the car. I almost recognized the voice. I was breathing hard.

"Come on over here. I won't hurt you."

Then I knew the voice. It was Damon Goodey, otherwise known as Damaged Goods. The lowest of the lowlife. I thought he'd left town.

I didn't walk toward him, but I didn't walk away, either.

"Like my car?" he asked.

I couldn't see Goodey. I was just talking to a shadow inside a car. A shadow and a cigarette. "I seen better," I said.

"Hey. It runs. And pretty soon I'll get a better one, too. You'll see."

As far as I knew, he'd never had a car before. Or a job. He couldn't even keep his shoes tied. I said, "So what do you want?"

"I been wondering where your father is."

"What's it to you?"

"He ain't working at the quarry. He ain't coming to the bar. Seems like nobody's seen him."

"He's busy."

"He's *gone*."

"You don't know."

"He's gone, and you're hungry."

"I just ate."

"You're still hungry, Danny. You're hungry for more than just food. You got *the hunger*. I know because I been there myself. And I found a way out. You can, too. And I think I can help."

"How?"

"You need a job. Right?"

"Dsh."

"Right, Danny?"

"I suppose."

The cigarette waggled. He said, "I think I can give you a job."

"Doing what?"

"Delivery."

"Deliver what?"

"The goods. You know I got the goods."

Yeah. *Damaged* goods, I think to myself.

Drugs.

I don't say another word to Damon Goodey. I walk away, then break into a run after I'm far enough so he won't think I'm running because I'm scared of him. Which I ain't.

So now I know how Damon Goodey got the money to buy a car. If I worked for him, I could buy a car, too, even if I ain't old enough to drive. I could buy a bike with gold handlebars, with eighteen forward gears and another three in reverse.

I could go to the restaurant for pizza every night.
I could get the TV repaired.

I could buy a chain saw.

At the store I stopped and called collect to
Tommy.

"Hey, Danny, you okay?" he said.

"Dsh."

"You got somebody taking care of you?"

"Yeah." Meaning, myself. "I even been offered a
job."

"Really? That's great."

"Uh. Tommy? How's Pop?"

"Better."

"But he's still crazy?"

"No, Danny. He's sick."

"He's still nuts?"

"He isn't nuts, Danny. Never was. It's called post-
traumatic stress disorder."

"What's that?"

"It means he saw too much war, too close up. It
happens. It stays with you when you go back to
the world. Even Audie Murphy had to sleep with
the lights on and a loaded gun by his bed."

"Who's Audie Murphy?"

"War hero. World War Two. The *good* war."

The way Tommy said *good*, I knew he didn't think
any war could be.

I asked, "Is that why Pop was so angry?"

"Yes. And moody. That happens. But he knew he
had a problem. That's the good thing. You can't

help somebody until he recognizes that there's a problem. That's why he went up in that tree. He's fighting it, Danny. He's gonna win, too. I was just talking to one of the nurses there. She's taking a personal interest in your father's case. She likes your father. Likes him a lot."

Well, I think to myself, I've got a personal interest in his case, too. Because I like him, too. I like him a lot. And I'm not sure I want that nurse's interest to get *too* personal.

I walk home in moonlight. As I'm passing the hill with the graveyard on top, I see movement on the hillside. Coyote movement?

I wonder, will Whiteknight find them? Should I chase them away?

Part of me says yes, I should try to help them. But part of me says they can take care of themselves. They're street. Probably just from smelling Whiteknight's pee they know all about him — what he eats and where he scratches.

Halfway up the hill there's a boulder. One coyote's on top of the boulder, the other's trying to climb. The one on top snaps at the other, chases it back or slams a hip into its body to knock it down.

I stand in the road and watch.

They're playing a game: king of the boulder. First one on top, then the other. Like a couple of kids.

Suddenly across the silent sky I see a shooting star. I yell, "Money money money!" fast because

everybody knows if you can say "money" three
times before the meteor disappears, money will
come your way. I can't tell whether I said it fast
enough or not. Sometimes you need an umpire.

When I look back at the boulder, the coyotes are
gone. They slipped off into the grass. I scared them,
screaming about money. They must think I'm crazy,
standing on a road, shouting at a shooting star.
Maybe I am.

In the farmyard I stop and check the coop. My
boards are still covering the hole. Probably the
coyotes won't try again even if I don't repair the
fence — not after Hoggle shot at them. And not
with Whiteknight as the new guard dog.

In the trailer I open my grammar book to the
next chapter and lay it under my pillow. I lie on
my bed with my head on the pillow, waiting for
words, waiting to learn.

I woke up with my fists clenched and my heart
pounding. I'd had another dream: Big Al with a
knife, coming to my bed after lights out, saying, *I'll
cut you. This time I'll cut the whole ear off.*

Only a dream. But it really happened, sort of like
that. He really said that. And he had a knife until
they found it.

Big Al would beat up a kid just for the fun of it.

I would've expected to be dreaming about grammar, since I was sleeping on the book. But the brain
works in mysterious ways.

I ran up the driveway just in time to meet Hoggle coming out of the chicken coop with a handful of eggs.

Drat. I was too late to collect them myself — and keep a couple for breakfast. My belly grumbled a complaint. I tried to tell it to be quiet, that I had five dollars in my pocket from selling baseball cards. I could buy something on the way to school.

I saw Whiteknight lying in the dirt with his fur full of stickers. He didn't even get up to growl at me. He looked exhausted.

Hoggle smiled at Whiteknight. "Looks like he's been chasing coyotes all night," he said. "That's what he's here for. But we gotta fix that coop, Danny. We gotta dig a trench and bury the wire."

"We?" I was thinking, 'What you mean *we*, white man?' Old joke.

"You," Hoggle said. "You gonna work today? Or do I have to sit out here all night with a shotgun?"

"I'll work. I would've done it yesterday, but I had to change your oil."

"Yeah. That. My wife tells me she paid you eight dollars."

"Maybe. I don't remember."

"We made a deal for six."

"Was it? I forget. Well, well. I guess you got a bargain. But you see, I had some problems."

"Like what? Roots?" Hoggle laughed. "Too many roots in that Ford?"

"Yes, sir." I smiled. "Lot of roots."

Then I ran.

At the store I bought a bag full of jelly doughnuts and ate three of them on the way to school.

Just as I got in sight of school while I was sucking the last sugar off my fingers, I dropped the grammar book. Bad news! That meant I'd forget everything I learned by sleeping on it unless I kissed the book before I picked it up.

I looked around. I hoped nobody was watching. I bent down on my knees and, quick as possible, kissed the front of the book. Then I sprang to my feet.

"Gee, Danny, you must really love English." It was Geraldine. Hairball. Smiling, maybe laughing at me.

"Shut up," I said.

"You want me to tell Mrs. Rule you got down on your hands and knees to kiss your English book? She'd be impressed."

"Don't tell *nobody*."

Geraldine was still smiling. Her eyes were twinkling.

I wondered if I could beat her up. She's six inches taller than me, not counting the hair. Something in her eyes reminds me of the coyotes. Something wild.

"Geraldine. Please."

"What's in the bag?"

"Doughnuts. Want one?"

"Thank you."

"Take two."

"Thank you."

"You gonna tell?"

Her face got serious. She said, "Don't worry. I wouldn't do anything to hurt you, Danny. Ever."

Then she walked away, eating a doughnut.

I never knew what to expect from Geraldine.

"Hey, Danny!" It was Babcock. He came running over to me. Babcock — running! When he reached where I was standing, he said, "What's in the bag?"

"Nothing," I said.

"You gave something to Geraldine. She was *eating* it."

I looked in Babcock's eyes. He was hungry. I ought to know how it feels. His diet was killing him.

"Have a doughnut," I said.

Babcock reached in the bag and took out two jelly doughnuts. The first he ate in one single bite. The second, he took two bites.

"Hey, Danny, whatcha got there?" It was Dylan.

"Can I have another?" Babcock said.

"Hi, Danny." It was Boone.

In a few minutes the doughnuts were gone. And so was my five dollars.

In English class, Mrs. Rule was talking about contractions. "Danny," she said, "what is the contraction for 'You are not'?"

Easy. "You aren't," I said.

"And Danny, what is the contraction for 'I am not'?"

"I'm not."

"Good. And what is the contraction for 'He does not'?"

"He . . . doesn't."

"Very good. Now, Danny, why is it that you can give me these answers on a test, but you don't want to talk that way?"

"I ain't sure exactly."

"Danny! Do you want to sound ignorant all your life?"

"That's how Pop talks."

"That's how my mother talked, too. Danny. Because she didn't know any better. But I have an education. And you have one, too."

"I can write it your way, Mrs. Rule. But when I say it your way, it don't sound right."

"*Doesn't*, Danny. It *doesn't* sound right."

"I'm glad you agree, Mrs. Rule."

Babcock cheered. Dylan clapped his hands. Boone looked shocked. Geraldine laughed. You might say I was the winner. But then you might not. Because Mrs. Rule decided I should stay after school and write two hundred times, "I'm not going to speak incorrectly. It doesn't sound right."

By the time I wrote it for the two hundredth time, I was thinking: She's right. It doesn't sound right. I ain't gonna talk ignorant. I mean, I'm not going to talk that way. Not no more.

Staying after school made me late starting work on the chicken coop.

The plan was to dig a trench and bury the chicken wire so the coyotes couldn't get under it. With a pick I dug halfway around. The soil was rocky, hard, dry.

I didn't like the idea of working against the coyotes, but I figured they wouldn't try to steal any more chickens, anyway, after being shot at last time. And I needed the money.

I got blisters. I sweated. My arms got tired, and they started to shake. My fingers kept trying to let go of the pick. I must've drunk a gallon of water from the hose.

And it was only half dug.

I dropped boards in the trenches, as the sun fell into the trees. Whiteknight finally seemed rested up after sleeping all day. He stretched, put his nose high in the wind, then trotted off behind the barn and out of sight. I stapled new chicken wire to the boards and tied it into the fence with baling wire. After dark, I shoveled the dirt back into the trench, and my blisters all popped.

Half done. But that was all I could do for one day. My arms were too tired and my hands were too sore. Now what about dinner? I could grab a chicken from the coop, take it home, and cook it —

and blame it on the coyotes. But I ain't that desperate. I mean, I'm not. If I'm desperate, Damon
Goodey can give me a job. But something tells me,
once I take that job, I'm climbing in a car that's got
no brakes.

I ain't — I mean, I'm not — that desperate.

Hear me?

I am not.

I walk to Boone's house. They've already eaten,
but Boone invites me in and finds excuses to give
me food: He asks his mother if we can make popcorn, and she says yes, and then he asks if we can
have a Hershey bar, and she says yes, and Boone
gives it all to me. So for dinner I have a bowl of
popcorn and two Hershey bars. Walking home, my
belly starts complaining.

I wish I could catch ground squirrels like a coyote. Then I could eat.

Where are the coyotes? I know I won't hear them
scuffling under the trailer anymore. They can't live
that close to Whiteknight.

I hope they stay out of trouble.

The smell of the wind coming off the pasture,
thick with grass and the coming of rain, just that
smell is enough to make my stomach growl. The
world is full of food. And I have none.

10
BANKRUPT

Next day after school I dug the rest of the trench. I grew blisters on top of blisters. It hurt so bad, I had to find a rag and wrap my hands, just so I could hold the pick.

But I got it dug. I installed the new chicken wire, filled the trenches, and I was done. To my surprise, it only took an hour and half today, which was the same as yesterday. It felt like ten hours. My hands looked like somebody shredded them.

But it was done.

I knocked on the farmhouse door. Hoggle answered.

"I finished, Mr. Hoggle."

"Good, Danny."

"It took three hours."

"Okay. Lemme see. Oh yeah. Here's seven dollars."

"*Three* hours, Mr. Hoggle. Times three dollars."

"Hmm. Yeah. But you took an extra two dollars from my wife, yesterday."

"No givebacks, Mr. Hoggle. It's a done deal. You said, 'Never no givebacks.' "

"Danny."

"Yes, sir?"

"Shut up."

But he gave me nine dollars.

I ran down to the store.

First thing my eyes light on is jelly doughnuts. Right next to them is a box of Ding Dongs. I grab them both. That takes care of the main course. A pack of Pepsis for my thirst. Then I have enough money left for some dessert: two Sugar Daddies and six red hots.

In line behind me, waiting to pay, was Walt.

"What happened to your hands, Danny?" Walt asked.

"Blisters," I said. "They popped."

"Don't they hurt?"

"Sure do."

"You need to cover them. Put some ointment on them, then wrap them up in a bandage."

"Yeah. I suppose."

Walt looked at me sharply. He knows my father. He knows we're poor. Even without knowing that Pop was in the hospital, he could figure the chances of me having the right first aid supplies in my trailer.

Walt said, "You've got a soccer game Saturday, Danny, and I don't want you to be distracted because your hands hurt. Come on back to my house, and I'll wrap you up. You're my striker, Danny. I need you healthy. And what's that crap you're buying?"

"Oh," I said, "just a snack." Suddenly I felt stupid. I should've bought milk. Bread. Bologna. Before Walt could give me a lecture on eating, I said, "Hey, Walt, I found us another player. Another Slime."

"Is he good?"

"He's never played."

"Never? Where's he been? In jail?"

"No. He's rich."

I rode to Walt's house on the back of his Harley-Davidson motorcycle with my grocery bag smashed between us. I wished the trip was longer, but it's a small town.

Walt rides that Harley over the hill every day to work in the valley. He's a new clear fist. At least, I think that's what he said. He says it's sort of like my father's job at the quarry. Except where my father smashes rocks, Walt smashes atoms. But Walt doesn't come home dirty like Pop.

First thing, Walt greased up my hands and then wrapped them with gauze and tape.

Dylan was watching. He said, "You look like the mummy from the crypt."

I said, "I feel like one, too." Because I felt like I hadn't eaten for a thousand years.

Then Walt asked the one question I didn't want to hear: "Where's your father, Danny? I haven't seen him at the bar all week. Is he all right?"

"He's okay," I said. I tried to act casual. "He's been busy."

"Are you sure he's all right? He was acting sort of . . . *moody*."

"He's okay."

"I've never known your father to miss an entire week at the bar."

"He quit drinking."

"Really? Well, well."

I could see he didn't believe me. But he didn't say anything more about it. What he did do is give me a uniform to take to Law so he could come dressed for the game, and then he gave me a ride on the back of his Harley to Law's house.

"Uh — Walt? Let me off at the end of the driveway."

Out of sight of the house.

Something told me Mrs. Livermore might not like the idea of Law playing for a coach who had a beard and traveled on a Harley.

After Walt roared away on his motorcycle, standing with the grocery bag and Law's uniform in my arms in front of Law's house with lights on in the windows and not a sound escaping to the outside, I became aware of how calm it was. How quiet.

How solid. Nobody was crowded on top of anybody else. Nobody was worried about where the next meal was coming from or how to stop the roof from leaking. No cars were blocking the driveway — they were safe and out of sight in the three-car garage: two Jaguars, **XLNT** and **I ERND IT**, and a Ping-Pong table (**XRCISE**?). Outside was a big flat yard, one of the few flat yards in San Puerco. Even the trees seemed more solid here. The air smelled rich with moisture and oxygen and money. Got too many slugs in the yard? No problem. We'll just build a swimming pool and cover the rest of the yard with concrete. Need soccer cleats? No problem. We'll just go to the store and buy them. Nobody even asked how much it would cost.

Mrs. Livermore answered the doorbell. She was holding a cocktail glass. I guess I looked clean enough. She told me to take off my shoes and come in.

"Law's cleaning his room," she said. "Do you know where it is?"

I looked around. I saw doors and hallways and a stairway and white carpet.

"No, ma'am," I said. "I'm afraid I'm lost."

"I'll take you."

She led me first to a bar where she said she wanted to "freshen up" her cocktail glass, and then we went up the stairs and down a hall to a door — with a deadbolt lock. She knocked.

"Who is it?" Law's voice asked from inside.

"Your friend Danny has brought something for you."

"Okay. Go away, and I'll open the door."

"Remember what I told you, Law? Clean up that room before dinner."

"I remember."

Mrs. Livermore walked down the hall and out of sight.

I heard the lock click open from the inside. The door opened, and there stood Law in a room with no floor. That is, if it had a floor, you couldn't find it under all the papers and boxes and shoes and books and clothes and magazines and parts of a model train and pieces of electronic equipment and empty soda cans and batteries and a Monopoly board and a model dinosaur and a bunch of CDs. It looked as if somebody had turned the room upside down and shook it — except for two things. There was a computer sitting on a desk with the screen glowing green, and there was a big glass-fronted cabinet full of baseball cards: stacked, labeled, and in perfect order.

Law locked the door behind me.

"I brought your uniform," I said. "Sorry about the color. They're all like that. Did you get cleats?"

"I wasn't sure which kind to get."

"So you don't have any?"

"I bought two pairs. One of each kind."

"Dsh."

"What?"

"Nothing."

"You want to see my baseball cards?"

I shrugged. "Okay."

The cabinet was locked, too. He opened it with a key.

"Don't touch them," he said.

"My hands are clean."

"What are all the bandages for?"

"Blisters."

"How'd you get blisters?"

"Working."

"Working gives you blisters?"

"Uh-huh."

"Oh."

I guess Law knew as much about working as I knew about being rich: nothing.

"Why can't I touch the cards, Law?"

"It wears them out. I never handle them."

"Don't you ever turn them over so you can read the batting averages and stuff?"

Law looked puzzled. "What for?"

"What for? What do you have the cards for?"

"I collect them. I don't *read* them."

"But what do you *do* with them?"

"I chart them on the computer. I keep track of their value. It keeps changing, you know. I get an update, and I have to rechart all the cards. Plus I have to add in any new ones that I get. Like those cards I got from you. Want to see them on the computer?"

Law typed some commands.

On the screen appeared a list of the cards.

"What's it mean?" I asked.

Law pointed at a line. "The first number's the year that the card was made. This one's 1954. Then the name of the card company. This one's Topps. Then that next number, 245, is the number of the card. Then Roy Sievers is the name of the player. G means it's in good condition. And the last number is the value of the card."

"Roy Sievers is worth a dollar twenty?"

"If the card was in better condition, he'd be worth twelve dollars. Where'd you get those cards, anyway?"

"From Boone. He's a friend of mine. He's on the soccer team. You'll meet him tomorrow."

"How much did you pay him for those cards?"

"Nothing."

"Nothing?"

"They were duplicates. He gave them to me."

"Where did *he* get them?"

"From his father's old collection."

"So he has *more*?"

While we were talking, I was reading the value of the rest of the cards I'd sold to Law for five dollars. A dollar ninety for one, sixty-five cents for another, a dollar sixty, two twenty-five, one forty, and on and on. And I was thinking: That makes *twice* I was hosed last time I came here.

"I've got some new games," Law said, pointing to some computer disks. "You want to play, Danny?"

"Don't you think you better clean up this room first? I'll help you."

"It can wait," Law said.

First we played some kind of car wars game. We each had a joystick. And he killed me. Totally destroyed me.

"Play again," he said. "I'll play left-handed."

So we played again, and he beat me just as bad.

"Try again," Law said, "I'll keep both hands behind my back."

"How will you move the joystick?"

"With my toes."

So he did. And killed me.

"All right," Law said. "I'll play you blindfolded."

"How can you play blindfolded?"

"I can hear it."

So I blindfolded him. And I knew he couldn't see out because it was tight and double-wrapped.

Law groped around with his hands until he found the joystick.

"Nuh-uh," I said. "Use your toes."

So we played. Blindfolded, with his toes, he killed me.

"This ain't — isn't — playing," I said. "This is total *demolish*."

"Dinner!" It was Mrs. Livermore's voice, outside

the door. "Law, is your room straight?"

"I'm not quite finished," Law called through the door.

"Let me see," Mrs. Livermore called.

Law said, "I'll finish right after dinner."

"Let me *see*."

"No."

"You won't *have* any dinner," Mrs. Livermore said. "Not until you straighten up to the point where I can see your room. Danny? Have you already eaten? Or would you like to join us for dinner?"

"I might have a few bites," I said.

I walked over the white carpet down the hallway, following the smell of steak and baked potatoes in the air.

As soon as I sit down I grab a glass of milk and pour it straight down my throat until it's gone with a few drops dribbling down my chin. Then I cut off a big hunk of steak and slam it into my mouth, and cut another and stuff it in there before I finish chewing the first one so my cheek bulges out and I can't even close my lips, and I cut another and happen to look up and see that Mrs. Livermore was just sitting there with her fork halfway to her mouth, staring at me.

"Hungry, Danny?" she said.

"A little. I — uh — I'm not used to eating so late."

Mr. Livermore was looking at me, too. Like he'd look at a big hairy spider.

I slowed down. Mr. and Mrs. Livermore drank red wine with the meal. Mr. drank three or four glasses; Mrs., one. I drank two more glasses of milk, ate another slab of steak, and helped myself to one and a half baked potatoes.

Mrs. Livermore with the blonde hair and blue eyes, the diamond earrings, and fancy dress looked to me like a movie star. She could've been dressed for the Oscars instead of just for dinner. Mr. Livermore had dark hair and one of those faces that always look like they need a shave. Next to her he looked old and tired and angry. His shoulders slumped forward, and his jaw looked like concrete.

When Mr. Livermore finished eating, he leaned back in his chair. "Well, Norma," he said, "I spoke with that man Henry Hoggle, and he said he could begin work on the pool tomorrow."

"Tomorrow?" Mrs. Livermore said. "My, that's quick. Oh, this is *excellent*."

Mr. Livermore nodded his head and said, "It's a pleasure to speak to a man who's eager to *earn* his money." He looked at me. "Don't you think so, young man?"

"Yes, sir," I said, "I mean, what other way is there to get money?"

"Some people," Mr. Livermore said, "seem to think they can get money by *whining* for it. There's only one way to get ahead in this world, and that is to work for it. Work hard. It's a choice you make.

You can choose to be poor, or you can choose to be rich. You aren't going to choose to be poor, are you, young man?"

"No, sir. I'm not." Hear that? *I'm not.* Sitting at the Livermores' table with Mrs. Livermore wearing diamond earrings under a sparkling chandelier, I could talk right. It sounded right. I said, "I'm not going to be poor. I'm not going to make any more wrong choices."

Mr. Livermore raised his eyebrows. "You've made some already?"

"Well. One," I said. A big one. The first choice of my life. If you believe that stuff.

Mrs. Livermore smiled. "We're all entitled to one mistake, Danny," she said. "But be careful. There are a lot of temptations. Sometimes it's hard to stay focused on what you want."

"I can stay focused," I said. "It's not hard." Check it out: *It's not.* No more *ain't* for me. I was feeling like one classy dude.

Mr. Livermore sat leaning back in his chair, scowling. He spoke, not to me but to his wife: "The main temptation of the poor," he said, "is that they spend all their money as fast as they can get it. They get paid, and they go directly to a tavern. When I drive by that bar in town and I see all those decrepit old cars parked outside — and *motor-cycles* — I can't imagine what pleasure they see in there."

"They meet their friends there," I said.

"And spend all their money, no doubt," Mr. Livermore said.

"Not really. Pop goes there, and he doesn't drink half as much as you do."

Mr. Livermore winced.

Mrs. Livermore said, "Danny, that's not a nice thing to say."

Mr. Livermore went back to scowling. He leaned forward. "Don't mind what he says, Norma. He's just a little *urchin*."

I'd seen urchins washed up on the beach. They were purple with spiny things all over. I didn't know why he called me that. But I didn't like it.

"Well," Mrs. Livermore said with a smile that seemed to take a lot of work, "tell me about this soccer game you've roped Law into playing tomorrow. What is the name of your team?"

I coughed.

"What, Danny?"

"What is the name of your team, Danny?"

"I forget."

Mrs. Livermore looked at Mr. Livermore. Something told me she didn't believe me. But whatever she was thinking, she didn't say. And whatever Mr. Livermore was thinking, I didn't want to know. Calling me a sea urchin.

The funny thing was, I was taking a liking to Mrs. Livermore. She *meant* well. She could've brushed me off like a fly, but here she was feeding me dinner at her table and talking to me like she cared about

me and encouraging Law to be friends with me,
even though she didn't know — she couldn't even
imagine — the way I live. All she knew was that my
clothes were raggedy and my skin was brown —
two reasons for her to freeze me out of her life, if
she wanted to. But she didn't. The one who wanted
to was Mr. Livermore, I think. I guess that's what
he meant, calling me that name.

"Mr. Livermore," I said, "about what you were
saying — about earning money? Could I ask you a
question?"

"What is it, young man?" He looked uneasy.

"How did you earn the money for that car?"

"Oh. Well, you see, I was a Cee Eee Oh. That
means Chief Executive Officer. I was the boss. I ran
a company."

"You don't anymore?"

"Well . . . no. The company doesn't exist
anymore."

"You mean you quit?"

"No. The company quit. It went bankrupt."

"Bankrupt? Doesn't that mean it went broke?"

"Yes."

"That sounds like a dsh situation."

"I beg your pardon?"

"How can you get rich if your company goes
broke?"

Mr. Livermore frowned. He didn't answer.

Mrs. Livermore leaned forward and explained:

"You see, Danny, he didn't *own* the company. He just *ran* it."

"Norma," Mr. Livermore said, "it is not necessary to explain — "

"The boy wants to learn," Mrs. Livermore said. "You see, running a company is a very important job. So they pay you a lot of money."

"But if the company goes broke, doesn't that mean you didn't do your job right? Isn't it your job to *keep* the company from going broke? Why would they pay you — "

"That's enough!" Mr. Livermore said.

"Yes, Nathan," Mrs. Livermore said.

And they both poured themselves another glass of wine.

"So," I said, "the way to get rich is to run a company that goes bankrupt."

Mrs. Livermore shook her head, but she also smiled. Mr. Livermore just scowled.

"Going bankrupt," Mrs. Livermore said, "is very complicated. I never understood it myself."

"Then I guess I can't, either."

"Some day you will, Danny. When you learn more about business."

"That's what I'm trying to do."

"Good."

"I'm going to work hard and earn a lot of money and buy a car just like yours."

"Good, Danny." Mrs. Livermore looked pleased.

"We all should earn the money for the things we want."

"What about you, Mrs. Livermore? How did you earn the money for that car?"

"Me? Oh, well, I married Nathan."

"Is that like going bankrupt?"

Mr. Livermore pushed back his chair with a screech that made me wonder if he'd ripped the carpet. Mrs. Livermore raised an eyebrow and watched him leave the table.

She never answered my question.

After dinner I checked on Law. He still hadn't started cleaning. He was sitting at the computer, running little stick figures through a castle dodging knives and hatchets and ghosts that were making weird noises.

"You better clean this room," I said. "Your mother's gonna kill you."

"No she won't," Law said. "She'll send my stepfather. And *he'll* kill me."

"I don't think he likes me."

"Join the club."

"He called me a sea urchin."

"Why?"

"I don't know."

"Don't worry," Law said. "He doesn't like me, either."

"Really?"

"I hate him," Law said this calmly, as if it weren't important.

"But, Law, if he doesn't like you, and you hate him, then . . . I mean . . . why . . . what's he doing . . . here?"

"They're married, you know."

"Yeah, but — "

"Of course they fight all the time."

"Dsh."

"Yeah," Law said. "Exactly. Dsh."

Law wiggled a joystick and dodged a flying hatchet. I was feeling uncomfortable. I said, "What about your room?"

"What about it?"

"Don't you think you should clean it?"

"Yeah," Law said. He didn't look away from the screen.

"I'll help," I said, and I picked up part of a model train from the floor. "Where does this go?"

"Take it," Law said.

"I *am* taking it. Where do I *put* it?" Law's room was almost as big as my whole trailer — kitchen, bathroom, the works.

"Take it. Keep it," Law said. "I'm giving it to you."

I looked in my hand. It was a Sante Fe locomotive. Heavy, with a motor. HO gauge.

Law was nuts. I'd rather have a train set than play computer games. With a train you can *do* things. You can lay track. You can build houses and water towers and mountains and rivers. You can put in switches and lights and a freight yard and a loading dock. And then the train actually *moves*. Not just on a TV screen. It's *there*.

Or course, to run trains you needed space. Which I didn't have. And money. A locomotive won't work without tracks and a transformer and cars to pull.

Maybe Law would give me everything — the works. Maybe if I said the right thing . . . if I picked up the next piece of train and said where do I put this . . . or if I dropped a hint like, gee, this locomotive is real nice, but I can't use it without the other stuff . . . no, too obvious . . . or I kept coming back to Law's house every day for one piece at a time . . . but he won't need to clean it up every day because he'll never use it again. . . .

Dsh.

Double dsh.

Bulldsh!

Look at me. Standing around hoping Law will give me this and not want that. The coyotes are right not to take my muffin. To pee on my doughnut.

It's poison.

"No thanks," I said, and I set the locomotive back on the floor next to a pile of socks. "I ain't gonna take it."

I walked to the door. I said, "It looks like you ain't gonna clean this room. And I ain't hanging around to find out what happens."

That's right: I ain't.

Maybe if I lived in Law's big house with Law's big room with space for a train set and steak for dinner and new cleats whenever I wanted, maybe

I could talk right. Definitely I could talk right. It would *sound* right.

But I ain't bankrupt. I'm just poor.

I'm a *ain't* person. I live in a *ain't* trailer. I got a *ain't* father. He ain't got no phone or no car. And I ain't got no bicycle.

This is my name: Danny Ain't.

I walked home with my grocery bag.

Maybe my father didn't give me a lot of things, and maybe he acted crazy sometimes, but at least I *liked* him. With his stepfather around, no wonder Law stayed in his room. He was like a prisoner.

Damon Goodey was sitting in his little Volkswagen by the lake. Inside I saw the glow of a cigarette.

I walked in a wide circle around him. I didn't want to talk about that delivery job right then. I just might've said yes.

There was no sign of Whiteknight as I walked by Hoggle's house. He was out chasing coyotes, I guess. Or at least searching for them. That was his job.

I left the grocery bag on the front step outside the trailer and walked back out to the road and toward the rising moon. I climbed the fence. At the top of the hill I sat down on the grass, leaning back against a tombstone. All the valley was dark — the farmhouses, my trailer, the road.

I looked up at the stars. Just looking. Just sitting.

I got to try it. I open my mouth and out it comes: *Ow-oooooooo.* It echoes off the hill on the other side of the valley. I try again: *Ow-ow-oooooooo.*

I sit there and listen. The night seems better now. Fuller. Richer. More alive.

Then I hear it! Just once. *Yap yap ow-oooo.* From another hill.

I rear back my head and give my best howl. I want them to hear that I know lonesome. I know hungry. I know *ain't.*

I listen, but there's no answer. All I hear is some meadow mice dancing in the grass. But then after a few minutes I get a feeling I can't explain, and I know I ought to turn around. Slow.

I ease my head around.

There's the two coyotes sitting on their haunches, looking right at me.

I ease my body around to catch up with my head.

I'm thinking, if we're going to be howling partners, I ought to know your names.

The female stands up. She yawns and makes a sound like *a-rool.*

All right, I decide. Your name is Miss Arool.

The male stands up, too. But he makes no sound. He wanders over to a madrone tree and rubs his back against the bark, scratching a flea bite. When he's finished, he shakes his head — and sneezes with a snorting noise that sounds like Hoggle's pickup truck when it won't start. So I decide his name is the General. General Mess. Pleased to meet you, General Mess.

"And my name's Danny Ain't," I say.

The sound of my voice startles them. They recoil backwards, then stare at me cautiously.

All I do is yawn.

They seem satisfied. The General wheels around and trots off into the high grass. Arool follows at his tail. In a moment, they've disappeared.

I'm satisfied, too.

It's warm out tonight. I lay back in the soft grass. I'm waiting for a shooting star, but instead, I fall asleep.

11
SHOES AIN'T POISON

I woke on the hill at sunrise to a dream about Big Al shooting coyotes and nailing their dead bodies to a wall.

I hate sleeping. If I never slept, I'd never have those dreams. I rolled over and felt cold wet dew on my cheek from the grass.

It felt fresh.

On a bed of dewy clover I rubbed both sides of my face, then washed with my hands. The dewdrops in my eyes cleared away all the bad dreams of the night.

I sat up and stretched and saw spiderwebs sparkling in the rising sun. Down in the valley, Hoggle's rooster was crowing. Up above, a red-tailed hawk was cruising, circling in an updraft.

The real world looked a whole lot nicer than the one I slept in.

I wandered toward home.

Back at the trailer, I found a mess. My grocery bag was dragged off the front steps and ripped to shreds in the yard. They tore open the doughnuts, leaving nothing but crumbs. They tried the Ding Dongs, too, but I guess they didn't like them. I couldn't find one of the Sugar Daddies or two of the red-hots. The Pepsis were okay.

So that was how it worked: coyote business. They wouldn't touch it if I gave it to them. That would be poison. But if I was careless — if I was *stupid* — if I left it out by *mistake* — then they wanted it. They *grabbed* it.

At school Boone was excited. "Tomorrow's the big day," Boone said. "The big soccer game."

"Yeah," I said. "Our first game of the year."

"No, it's our second," Boone said. "But it's our first as coaches."

I realized then that Boone wasn't talking about our own team's game. He was looking forward to coaching the Noodledoods, which Mr. Barnaby had put us in charge of because he had to be out of town.

"Think they're ready?" I asked.

"No," Boone said. "I don't think they have a clue."

"Me, neither."

"But it's going to be *fun*."

I wasn't so sure.

Saturday morning I got a ride with Boone and his mother in their Volkswagen bus. We played our games over the hill in a suburb called Pulgas Park because there weren't enough kids in San Puerco to make a league. We could just barely make a team.

Before the game all the Noodledoods were scampering around. Besides Boone and myself, Dylan and Geraldine and Babcock had arrived already to help as assistant coaches. Walt was there, too, and when he saw me he wandered over and said, "Are you ready? Have you got cleats? Shinguards?"

I was wearing my sneakers with duck tape wrapped around them.

"I got cleats," I said. "I just haven't put them on yet."

"Tight?"

"A little. But they work."

"Last year's?"

"And the year before."

Walt looked pained, as if the shoes were pinching his toes instead of mine. "I'll *bet* they're tight," he said. "They must really *pinch*."

"Nope," I said. "They don't pinch because of the holes."

"But when you kick, Danny, doesn't it hurt your toes?"

"I don't kick with my toes, you know. Like you taught me. And having my toes out there, it helps to remind me."

"Remind you what?"

"That if I kick with my toes, it hurts. So I don't. And that's good. Right, Coach?"

"But — Danny, those cleats must be worn down to nubs by now. You won't have any traction."

"Hey. I can play."

Walt said he'd just remembered something he forgot to bring to the game, and he zipped off in his car. He didn't ride the motorcycle to games because he had to bring Dylan and a bunch of soccer balls and a big first-aid kit.

There was a playground next to the field, and some Noodledoods were climbing the jungle gym in their cleats. Then they ran out on the field, and Clover, Boone's little sister with dimples and curls and pink shoelaces, little Clover the size of a salami, ran out yelling, "Let's go, Noodledoods! Let's kick some *butt!*"

Boone, carrying a clipboard, and myself and Geraldine, Babcock, and Dylan tried to get the Noodledood players lined up to begin the game.

Clover had sounded ready to play ball. And she was — for about two minutes. She was goalie. A couple minutes into the game I looked down there, and she'd wandered out of the goal to talk to Brian, the fullback. She was standing with her back to the play.

I ran down to the end of the field and yelled, "Hey Clover! Get back in front of the goal!"

She didn't even look at me. She was talking, and then she bent down. Brian got down on his knees. They were pulling up handfuls of grass. Brian's got a big mop of curly hair on his head.

Geraldine the Hairball came down the side of the field to where I was standing. Brian is her little brother. You can tell by the hair.

Dylan tagged along after Geraldine. He followed her like a puppy.

"What are they doing?" Geraldine said.

"Gardening," I said.

"HEY BRIAN!" she yelled. "GET UP!" Geraldine's got a voice that could stop a train.

They didn't hear.

Dylan tried. "Brian!" Dylan yelled. "Clover! Pay attention!"

They didn't hear. Dylan's voice doesn't carry.

The ball came rolling toward them.

"BRIAN!" Geraldine yelled. She stuck her hands in her ball of hair. Somehow that gave her the power to shout even louder. "BRIAN! KICK THE BALL!"

There were three soccer games playing right then on three different fields. Everybody from all three games — players, refs, parents — *everybody* stopped and looked at Geraldine. Everybody, that is, except two people.

Clover and Brian went right on pulling grass.

The ball rolled, slowly, losing speed, right past them and just made it into the goal, where it stopped dead.

Geraldine turned around and punched me in the arm.

"Ow!" I said.

"Oh. Sorry," she said. "That *stupid* kid. Wait'll I get in the car with him."

Boone walked onto the field. I listened for what he'd say. If I went out there, I'd say, "What are you? Noodlebrains?" But Boone's father wanted us to do positive coaching. So what could Boone say?

He bent over where Clover and Brian were still pulling up grass and said, "What are you doing?"

Clover looked up. "We're feeding a gopher," she said.

Boone examined the gopher hole and the pile of grass that they'd picked. He said, "I think he's got enough, now."

"You think so?" Clover asked.

"We don't want him to get *fat,*" Boone said. "You'd better stop for a while. You can give him some more grass after the game."

"Okay," Clover said, and she walked back into the goal.

The Noodledoods kicked off.

A minute later, Clover wandered out of the goal area. She was talking to Brian again. Brian giggled.

"Uh-oh," Geraldine said, and she ran down the side of the field.

Dylan ran after her.

Clover leaned forward and kissed Brian on the cheek. Brian giggled again. The ball was rolling their way.

Geraldine yelled, "BRIAN! WAKE UP!"

This time he heard. He looked around. He saw the ball rolling toward him. He fell to his knees, put out his hands, and caught it. A perfect stop. Except he forgot one thing. He was the fullback, not the goalie.

Geraldine screamed. An old man beside me turned off his hearing aid. I stepped away before she could hit me again. She hit Dylan instead. He looked puzzled, but he didn't complain. At least she paid some attention to him.

The ref blew the whistle.

The other team got a penalty kick, which nobody on either team seemed to understand, but finally the ref got it organized, and they kicked a goal.

"Brian," Boone said, "I think I'd better put you away from Clover. You go up as a forward."

"Where's that?" Brian said.

"Up here. On the line."

"Oh. Okay." But he looked puzzled. He said, "What do I do?"

Babcock stepped forward. He got down on his knees and looked Brian in the eye. "Kick the ball," he said.

"Oh."

"Don't use your hands," Babcock said.

"Uh-huh."

"Okay, Brian?"

"Just stand there? And when the ball comes, I kick it?"

"Don't just stand there," Babcock said. "Run after it and kick it again. Keep doing that until you're close to the goal. Then kick the ball into the goal."

"Why?" Brian asked.

"Because we get a point," Babcock said.

"Oh," Brian said. "A point." He looked serious. "I want to get a point."

The Noodledoods kicked off. Brian got the ball. He kicked. He stopped for a moment and watched where the ball went. You could see the wheels turning in his head. It clicked. He ran after the ball. He kicked it again. He ran. Everybody on the side- lines was yelling at him. He didn't hear. His own team was yelling at him. He didn't hear. Geraldine the foghorn was yelling. He didn't hear. He kicked. He ran. He was all alone. He kicked again — right past Clover into the goal.

Everybody stepped away from Geraldine — even Dylan. She was kicking clods of dirt.

Babcock slapped his forehead.

Boone said, "Let me handle this." Then he smiled, sort of. "Very good, Brian," he said through his teeth.

Brian ignored Boone — and his sister Geraldine,

and me and Dylan and everybody else on the field — and ran straight to Babcock. "I did it," Brian said. "Didn't I do it, Babcock?"

Babcock again got down on his knees. He said, "That's the idea, Brian. But there's one thing I forgot to tell you. Next time, kick into the *other* goal."

"Did we get the point?" Brian said.

"No. The other team got the point."

"But you said — "

"You have to kick it in the other goal."

"Then do we get a point?"

"Yes."

"Okay. A point." Brian went back to the middle of the field.

The Noodledoods kicked off. Brian ran into a whole herd of players. A couple of bodies fell down on the ground, and Brian came out with the ball. He kicked. He ran. A fullback tried to kick. Brian plowed into him and kicked the ball. The fullback did a backward somersault, and his glasses fell off. The ball went into the goal.

Everybody was cheering. Suddenly I noticed how many people were watching this game. The thing is, San Puerco is such a long way from where we play our games that when a grown-up gives a kid a ride to the game, he usually stays to watch unless he's got some errands to run. It's too far to just drop the kid off, go home, come back, and pick him up like most of the parents for the other teams do, especially for the older kids. A lot of those kids walk to the game.

Today there were two games back to back — first the Noodledoods, then the Sucking Slime. Most of the parents of the Slime kids had arrived already, so there was a double crowd cheering for San Puerco. Cheering hard.

Brian heard the cheering. He might not hear big sister Geraldine shouting like firecrackers with her face turning red and veins popping out, but he could hear what he wanted to hear. He beamed. He ran to Babcock and asked, "Do we get a point now?"

"Yes, Brian. We get a point."

"Should I do it again?"

"Yes, Brian. Please."

The other team kicked off. Brian ran the ball down, shouldered one of his own Noodledood players out of the way, and booted it. He ran. He kicked.

"My God," Geraldine said. "We've created a monster."

Brian mowed down one of the opposing players and punched another goal.

More cheering. Brian grinned.

"Okay, Brian," Boone said. "I think you'd better go back to fullback now."

"Did we get a point?"

"Yes, Brian."

Brian played fullback. The other team kicked off.

Clover came out of the goal to tickle him. He giggled and stepped away. She giggled and stepped after him and tickled him again. He stepped away. They were moving toward the sideline where we were standing. The goal was completely undefended.

"BRIAN!" Geraldine yelled. She was practically in his ear. "KICK THE BALL!"

Brian ignored her.

"Brian," Babcock said. "Kick the ball."

Brian looked around. He saw the ball rolling toward the goal. He ran toward it, kicked, followed it, kicked again, elbowed a player in the face, kicked, ran down the sideline, kicked to the center of the field, plowed into a fullback, kicked — and scored another goal.

"Who'd of thunk it?" Geraldine said. "My sweet little brother."

After halftime, Boone put Brian in as goalie.

"Don't you want to win?" I asked him.

Boone said, "We should give somebody else a chance to touch the ball. Plus, I'm afraid Brian's going to *kill* somebody."

Brian stayed in front of the goal looking bored. Clover went over to talk to him. Pretty soon both of them were hanging by their hands like monkeys from the crossbar at the front of the goal, swinging back and forth.

Then the ball came.

Brian dropped to the ground. A player on the other team took a shot. The ball hit Brian dead-on in the face. He fell backward. The ball bounced back onto the field. Everyone stopped. They were looking at Brian to see if he was all right. He was lying on the ground. Boone ran out. So did Geraldine. Brian got up. He dusted himself off. He looked around. "Where's Babcock?" he said.

"I'm here," Babcock said from the sideline.

"I want to kick the ball," Brian said. He looked mad.

Boone and Geraldine came off the field. Play resumed. The same player who kicked the ball into Brian's face was getting ready to take another shot. Brian rushed out and *smashed* the ball. On the follow-through from his kick, Brian's leg caught the other player behind the knee and picked him up and tumbled him over. Brian didn't even glance at him. He chased after the ball — and stepped on the player who was down — and ran into a crowd of players — like a bowling ball going down the alley — and pins flew everywhere as Brian came out with the ball. Down the field he went. Kick. Goal.

The Noodledoods won, four to three. Brian scored five goals — four for us, one for them.

"I guess it runs in the family," Geraldine said, patting her hair.

Walt showed up just in time for our game. He was carrying a pair of soccer shoes. "Try these on, Danny," he said. "They might fit."

They fit okay.

"Where'd they come from?" I asked.

"Found 'em," Walt said.

They looked brand new. In fact, they still had a plastic string stuck in them where the price tag had been attached.

I looked at Walt.

"Keep 'em, Danny."

Shoes ain't poison.

"Thanks, Coach."

12
THE BADGER

The Slime played their first soccer game of the season, and Law played the first of his life. His mother didn't stay to watch. She arranged for Law to ride home with me — that is, with Mrs. Barnaby — and said she had an appointment and was already late, and she drove off in the **XLNT** Jaguar.

I played in my brand-new cleats, which I laced starting from the top because it always brings me good luck.

The Noodledoods had played on a dry field, but somebody had run the sprinklers on our field and it was wet. In fact, it was muddy.

Walt used Law as a halfback. Watching Law play, I realized something I like about soccer: It doesn't matter what kind of car you arrive in. There's no rich or poor. Just quick or slow.

From what Law had seen in the Noodledoods' game, he must have concluded that the way to win was to play like Brian. The trouble was, Brian was built like a bowling ball, while Law was built like a normal human being. Also, Brian was playing against six- and seven-year-olds, while Law was up against kids who'd been playing soccer for years. The first time Law got the ball, he tried to dribble it through an opposing player the way Brian had, but instead, the other player stole the ball and knocked Law back on his butt.

And Law got right back up again. Didn't even wipe the mud off his shorts.

The next time Law got the ball, he tried to dribble it again. This time, though, instead of approaching the player on the other team, he waited until the other player made a move to approach him, and then Law kicked the ball to the side and got around him. Meanwhile, I was shouting, "Man on!" to warn him that another player was coming up behind him, but Law didn't know what I meant and was taken by surprise by a slide tackle — and ended up on his butt. In the mud.

Law got right back up again. He looked at his shorts, saw the mud — and smiled.

I told Law to pass the ball, that only little kids tried to dribble the ball all the way down the field. So next time he got the ball, Law tried to pass to me. The trouble was, he toed it. Nobody had taught him how to kick the ball with the side of his foot.

With the toe he had no control and too much power. The ball sailed out-of-bounds.

A minute later, an air ball came my way, so I headed it. Law must have been impressed, because a few minutes later when a big booming punt from Babcock came his way, Law positioned himself under it and took it on the top of his head. The ball bounced straight up again, and Law staggered two steps to his right and collapsed into a heap on the ground. Nobody had told him you take a header on your forehead so you don't rattle your brains.

But, a second later, Law was on his feet again.

We won the game, two to one. Geraldine scored both goals, one on a setup from me, one on a penalty kick. Walt congratulated us, and then, rubbing his beard, he looked at Law. Mud covered Law's shorts and shirt, plus his arms, legs, and face. Nobody else on the team had nearly as much dirt on them. Of course, nobody else had fallen down as much. Once or twice, in fact, I'd had the impression that Law actually enjoyed falling down and rolling in the mud. Still rubbing his beard, Walt said, "You showed two things on the field today that I like, Law. You have speed, and you seem to want to play."

"Yes," Law said. "I do want to play."

"However," Walt said, "you need to spend more time on your feet and less on your butt. Come to practice next week. You need it."

"I'll be there," Law said. "That's a promise." Then

he turned to me. "Will you come home with me, Danny? We could have some lunch, and then you could teach me some things about how to play. We could practice in my yard. It's flat. It's like a soccer field."

Law said *lunch*. Naturally, I said, "Yes."

Suddenly Babcock was jostling my shoulder. "Hey! Me, too." He jumped in front of me and said to Law, "I could teach you some things."

"Okay," Law said.

Babcock, I realized, had heard the magic word, too.

Riding back to San Puerco in the Barnabys' Volkswagen bus, Law invited Boone to come help him learn to play soccer with me and Babcock. Boone said he couldn't. He had to build a house for his dog. Then Law said, "I hear you have a baseball card collection. Could I see it some time?"

Uh-oh, I thought.

"Sure," Boone said. "You can see it any time."

"I have a few cards myself," Law said.

I rolled my eyes.

"Sometimes," Law said, "I like to buy cards from other kids. Would you like to sell any?"

I shook my head, trying to warn him: *Don't get hosed, Boone.*

"I don't sell cards," Boone said.

I breathed a sigh of relief.

"I give them away," Boone said.

I wanted to scream.

"Really? Would you give me some?" Law said.

I formed the words *No* and *Don't* with my lips, but Boone wasn't looking. "I don't have any extras right now," Boone said. "Do you?"

"Who, me?" Law said. "Why would I — I mean — um — no."

"Then I guess you can't give me any, either," Boone said.

"Um — no," Law said, looking confused.

"Well, if you get any you want to give away, let me know," Boone said.

"Uh — okay," Law said.

Dealing with Boone can be strange, as Law was finding out. He not only plays everything fair, but also he expects — he just *assumes* — that you'll play fair, too. And the funny thing is, you usually do.

Mr. Barnaby dropped Law, Babcock, and me at Law's house. Standing in the driveway out of sight of the house, Law looked at his clothes and said, "Danny, I think I need to ask you a favor. If my mother sees me like this, she'll never let me play soccer again. How'd you manage to stay so clean?"

"I stayed on my feet."

"Will you do me a favor?"

"What?"

"The hose."

"It would be a pleasure."

Hosing Law on a warm afternoon wasn't quite

equal to being hosed on a cold windy evening, but it was close enough. Babcock was puzzled, though. He said, "Why doesn't he just use the bathroom?" So I explained about how they didn't want to get the bathrooms dirty, and how Mrs. Livermore wouldn't like seeing how muddy Law got playing soccer, and how Law had hosed me before. "Was it cold?" Babcock said. "Did it hurt?" So I told him how a cold wind had been blowing, and how I'd had to scrub with a brush.

Babcock got a gleam in his eye. "Give me the hose," he said. He held his thumb over the end and sprayed Law hard. He aimed at his feet and made Law dance.

"Why are you doing this?" Law said, hopping.

Babcock handed the hose back to me. "Now you're even," he said.

I rang the doorbell and got a towel from Mrs. Livermore.

"What does he need a towel for?" she asked.

"We — uh — we were playing with the hose."

Law wrapped himself in the towel, then went inside to put on clean clothes. When he came down from his room, Mrs. Livermore asked, "How do you like soccer, Law?"

"I *love* it," he said.

"Oh my," she said. "I mean, that's excellent that you like it. But I hope you took it easy, this first time. You don't want to strain yourself."

"I took it *hard*," Law said.

"Well, I hope you didn't hurt yourself."

"Not too much."

"Then you did hurt yourself? Where are you hurt? I'll call the doctor. Quick. Tell me."

"Just some bruises."

"Do they hurt?"

"Of course they hurt. That's what bruises are. They hurt."

"We'll go to the doctor and get some pills. You shouldn't have to hurt."

"Never mind. I don't want any pills."

"Law, I don't know whether I like the effect soccer seems to have had on you. You seem hostile. Maybe you should find some other game."

"No."

"What do you like about soccer?"

"It's real."

"It's a game, Law. It isn't real."

"Yes, it is. It's the most real I've ever felt."

Mrs. Livermore gave us sandwiches. Law told her he had to go to soccer practice next Tuesday.

"You can't," she said. "You have your drum lesson."

"I'll skip it," he said.

"You play drums?" I said.

"Used to," he said.

"I'll see if I can reschedule it," Mrs. Livermore said.

Law only ate half his sandwich. After I finished mine, I asked if he'd mind if I took the rest of his.

"I'll make you another," Mrs. Livermore said.

While she made it, Babcock ate the rest of Law's.

Law's yard was a flat grassy meadow — well, half grass and half brush and wildflowers. I remember before a house was ever there it was a natural meadow where the grass was always green, even in the summer when the grass on all the hills turned brown. It was as if the meadow had its own natural sprinkling system. It needed mowing, though, before it would make a good practice field for soccer. We trampled down one section so the ball could roll. A couple of slugs slipped out of our way.

Babcock leaned over and studied one of the slugs. "All your slugs have red spots," he said. "Usually they're just yellow."

"I've seen dozens," Law said. "They seem to like it here."

I was just beginning to show Law about kicking with the side of his foot when there was a clanking and a roaring in the driveway: Hoggle, bringing his old tractor on a trailer, pulled by a sad-looking old dump truck.

Law frowned.

"What's happening?" Babcock asked.

"Henry Hoggle," I said.

"The total destruction of my soccer field," Law said. "He's going to put in a swimming pool and a big concrete patio."

"And you don't want it?" Babcock said.

"No."

"And what are you going to do about it?"

"What *can* I do?"

Babcock stood still for a moment, thinking. Then he walked over to Hoggle. He studied the tractor up and down. The machine was so old, it was a wonder it ran at all. It looked like a rolling rust ball held together with baling wire and Elmer's glue.

Hoggle pulled me aside. "I want to thank you, Danny. For the referral. Jobs like this come once in a lifetime. You know what I mean?"

I knew what he meant. At least, I knew his motto.

"Are you Mr. Hoggle?" Babcock asked.

"That's right."

"Is that your tractor?"

"Yep."

Babcock was looking at the exhaust stack. It was broken in half, with pieces of metal flaking off. "Do you have a spark arrestor on that thing?"

Hoggle looked surprised. "Nope," he said. "They didn't require them back when I bought this guy. Bought it so I could dig pits to catch dinosaurs, you know."

Babcock wasn't amused. He said, "Do you know it's a state law? You can't operate one of these without a spark arrestor."

"That's only if the state finds out," Hoggle said.

"What about a backup beeper?" Babcock said. "Got one of those?"

"Nope."

"Do you have a grading permit for this job?"

Hoggle scratched his head. "What is this?" he said. "Twenty questions?"

Babcock folded his arms and said, "Either that machine goes, or I make some phone calls. The Department of Forestry will want to know about somebody operating without a spark arrestor. It's a fire hazard. The Occupational Safety and Health Administration will want to know about you not having a backup beeper. They write tickets for that. And the County Permit Department will want to know about grading without a permit. I understand there's a pretty big fine for that."

Now Hoggle looked mad. He's normally red, but now he looked redder. "You little *badger*," he snarled.

Babcock looked pleased. "Yep, that's me," he said. "Babcock Badger."

I had to admit, the name fit. We'd tried to nickname Babcock before, but the names never stuck. Even his parents never could get him to take another name. But nobody ever tried Badger before.

"You're a god damned *bureaucrat*," Hoggle said.

Babcock frowned. "No," he said, "I'm a badger. And I'll fight you any way I can."

That's what badgers do, you know. They're ferocious little beasts. They can kill a dog. Sometimes, though, they make friends with coyotes. You'll see a badger and a coyote working together, the badger digging at a hole, the coyote guarding the back door. Pop says he's even seen them walking across a field together, like buddies.

Hoggle went to the house. I saw him talking to Mrs. Livermore at the front door, waving his arms and looking angry. Mrs. Livermore listened calmly, sucking on a drink.

Hoggle came clomping back to his tractor. He glared at Babcock. He fired up the old dump truck — it coughed and belched and shook — and he drove it away, pulling the trailer.

Babcock said, "I don't believe those taillights work on his trailer." He filed that little piece of information away in his brain.

Law was staring at Babcock with a look of total awe.

Mrs. Livermore walked over to where we were standing. "What was that all about?" she said.

"Mother," Law said, "I don't want a swimming pool."

"Why not?"

"I want a soccer field. This yard is perfect. All we have to do is mow the grass."

"What is this sudden infatuation with soccer?"

"It's real."

"It's a *game*."

"It's a real game."

"I think we'd better talk to your father about this when he gets home."

"He isn't my father."

"Law!"

"He's my stepfather."

"He's like a father to you, and we're going to have to talk about this."

Mrs. Livermore went back into the house, and Law and Babcock and I kicked the ball around for the rest of the afternoon until Law's stepfather drove his **I ERND IT** Jaguar up the driveway. The garage door opened automatically, and he drove inside.

Law said, "You guys had better go now."

Much as I wanted to try to mooch dinner, I knew he was right. I didn't want to be part of the discussion that I figured was coming.

Babcock and I walked to the end of the driveway, then turned our separate ways. "So long, Badger," I said.

Babcock smiled. "So long, Danny," he said.

Maybe, I thought, he's finally got a name.

13
POISON

I ran home with an empty stomach. The sun was just going down, and pink bands of cloud were blowing overhead.

Goldie was dead to the world, sleeping under the porch. Whiteknight had already gone off on his nightly wanderings.

I sat on the steps outside the trailer, watching the clouds change to a deep red. Daydreaming. Thinking about pizza the color of the sky.

Somewhere in my daydream I get the feeling I'm being watched. I look around. Sure enough, the two coyotes are sitting on their haunches not thirty feet away, studying me like I'm some animal in a zoo.

When I meet their eyes, Miss Arool gets nervous. She skitters away into some bushes. But General Mess holds his ground. Still watching me, he bends his head and lifts his hind leg to scratch at a flea behind his ear. He scratches so hard, I expect his ear to fly off. Then he shifts to trying to scratch his belly, which puts him in such an awkward position that he starts leaning over and suddenly collapses to the ground in a heap of legs and fur. He makes a grunt like the sound of a rusty nail being pulled out of a board, and he stands himself up and shakes off the dust, shaking first from his head and then wiggling on back to his rear. He makes a regular dust cloud. His fur is rough, scruffy-looking.

Miss Arool comes back. She's got something in her mouth. She sets it down at the feet of General Mess. A dead rat.

The General looks at me. His tongue hangs out. He cocks his head to the side. He raises his front leg and paws it at the air toward me like he's ringing an invisible doorbell. He picks up the rat with his teeth and tosses it into the air, catching it in his mouth. Three times he tosses it. Then, looking right at me, he drops it. He lowers his front to the ground with his front paws out straight on either side of the rat. His rear is sticking up in the air. He's wagging his tail.

He wants to play!

He wants to play keepaway with a dead rat. I stand up. He looks at me cautiously. I don't want to grab a dead rat, but I doubt he'd let me get that close, anyway. I make a lunge in his direction. He looks delighted. With a big doggy grin he picks up the rat and scampers out of my reach.

Miss Arool stands off to the side, watching.

I stamp my foot toward the General, and he shoots off in a big circle out around the oak tree and back near me. I stamp again, and he takes off again in the same big circle, only cutting it just a little shorter this time.

I stamp.

He runs.

Again. And again. Each time the circle gets a little smaller.

Now he stands ten feet from me. He drops the rat at his feet and stands there, panting, tongue hanging, like he's saying, 'Thanks for the game.'

I take a step forward.

He snatches up the rat and runs over to Arool. She takes it from his mouth, sort of like she's annoyed with him. She trots a few feet away and eats it.

The General tiptoes over next to her and rubs his face against the side of her neck. She snaps at him. He jumps away, wagging his tail. Her tail gives a little blip in return.

He's forgiven. But not satisfied. He comes back and growls. Suddenly there's an explosion of growls and snarls and legs flying in the air, and in five seconds he's got her pinned with his teeth on her throat. For half a minute he holds her there. When he finally lets her up, she creeps over to him and barfs up the rat she just ate. The General stands over that pile of vomit like he's guarding a treasure and gives me a look that says, like, don't you *dare* try to steal this puddle of barf.

Then he eats it.

They set off walking toward the pasture. General Mess stops, looks back at me.

I take a step in their direction.

The General seems satisfied. He walks on.

I follow.

We walk along a fence-line that's overgrown with vines. General Mess walks in front, with Miss Arool a few feet back, and me way back.

Suddenly Miss Arool stops. So I stop. The General, for no reason I can see, leaps into the air. He whirls around. He's acting crazy. He snatches a piece of wood from the ground and tosses it up in the air. He staggers, like he's been shot. I'm wondering: Is he loco?

Arool, meanwhile, is creeping up on something. A bird. The bird is watching the General like it's fascinated. Hypnotized. It can't figure what this clown is up to.

Neither can I.

Now the General is leaping up and down and waving his tail. Totally bananas.

The bird and me, we both are staring at the General.

Then Arool pounces. On the bird.

Caught.

Immediately the General is all business. He drops

the clown act and rushes over to Miss Arool, and they rip the bird apart.

And, watching, I've learned a little more about coyote business: Be careful with clowns.

The clouds overhead are now a deep purple. A couple of cattle are bellowing in cow-talk.

Suddenly General Mess pricks his ears. Miss Arool lifts her nose to the wind. They study for a few seconds. Then they set off at a fast trot, and I don't try to follow. I don't know what they heard or smelled, but I know they sensed danger.

I cut across the field to the road. And there's the danger: Hoggle, unloading something from the bed of the pickup. He drags it into the field and lets go. It looks like part of a carcass.

"What's that, Mr. Hoggle?"

"Bait," he says.

"Is that a sheep?"

"Part of one. Burke gave it to me."

Burke's the sheep rancher who lives up the road.

"Is it poison?"

"You bet, Danny. I hope you don't have a taste for raw meat. Couple bites of this, and you'll be dead meat, yourself."

Hoggle wraps wire around the bait and ties it to a fence post.

"Mr. Hoggle? You're after coyotes, right?"

"Right."

"Why? They don't kill cattle."

"True."

"The chicken coop's fixed. So they won't get any more chickens."

"Probably not."

"Pop says all they eat is mostly rats and ground squirrels and rabbits and meadow mice. The same animals that eat your grass. You want to save the grass for the cattle, don't you? Coyotes eat the grass-eaters, so the cows can eat the grass."

"Burke lost a sheep."

"Maybe it was sick."

"It was run down, Danny. Burke found it a half mile from the flock. Bite marks all over. Didn't eat it, either. Just killed it for sport."

"Maybe it got sick and died. Maybe the coyotes found it dead. Maybe it wasn't coyotes at all. Maybe it was . . ."

"What?"

"Bear."

Hoggle laughs. "They shot the last bear fifty years ago. You a coyote-lover, Danny? You love them varmints?"

I don't answer.

"You want a ride back to the house, Danny?"

"No, thanks. I'd rather walk."

Hoggle drives away.

I want to untie the bait and haul it away, but if I do, Hoggle will know it was me. No animal could unwrap those wires.

How can I warn the coyotes? Here's a free meal,

fresh meat, easy pickings. A couple bites and they're goners.

I remember what they did when I left them a doughnut. Maybe that's their warning signal. It's worth a try.

I wet it down, as much as I can, to the very last drop. Then I walk home. I sleep a bad night, even worse than usual.

Soon as there's daylight I'm up and running along the road. I find the sheep bait and two dead crows. In the dust I see paw prints, so I know the coyotes checked it out.

Was it my warning? Probably not. If they wouldn't eat a gift from me, likely they wouldn't eat one from Hoggle.

A turkey vulture circles overhead. He'll die, too, just like the crows. And if a skunk or a porcupine or even somebody's house cat comes along and eats the dead birds, that animal will die, too.

Maybe even the ants and flies will die.

Poison is stupid. It don't care who it kills. It just kills.

14
U.S. GRANT

So it was Sunday morning with the sun just barely peeping over the side of the mountain. The coyotes weren't poisoned. And I was still hungry.

It didn't seem fair. Every day I fed my belly, and next day did it remember? No. It just said, *Feed me today*.

Hoggle wasn't up yet. I gathered eggs for him and left them in a cardboard box on his front porch by the door — and kept two for myself. Goldie was sound asleep, of course, and Whiteknight came staggering home as I was leaving. He looked like he'd been chasing coyotes all night through burrs and foxtails and spiderwebs. He plopped himself down with a grumpy sound, dropped his head on his paws, and he was out.

I fried the two eggs for breakfast.

There wasn't one other crumb of food in the trailer. Two pennies in my pocket.

I went down to the store and called Tommy.

He sounded sleepy when he answered the phone: "Hoo-yum. Yeah yeah. I'll accept the call. Hi, Danny. They taking care of you?"

"Yeah."

"So you've got everything you need?"

"No problem."

And as I'm saying 'No problem,' I'm wondering why am I saying this? But I say it. I always say it. I knew a girl once whose mother was a drunk, and nobody knew it because the mother stayed home drunk where nobody could see her and the girl never said one word about it, and the worse things got at home, the harder that girl tried to make everything seem okay until one day the mother got so sick, they had to take her in an ambulance to a hospital. When people asked her later why she hadn't told anybody she had a problem, the girl just shook her head. And nobody understood what she meant, except me.

"Tommy? Is Pop ready to come home?"

"No. Well. Yes and no."

"What does that mean?"

"He's already halfway out. He's an outpatient. That means he doesn't sleep in the hospital, and that's good because it's kind of weird in there. But they want him to come back and talk every day, and since he doesn't have a car and you know how far it is, he's rooming in a house."

"So he's better?"

"Much better. Remember I told you there was a nurse at the hospital who was taking a personal interest in his case? Well, he's taking a personal interest in her case, too."

"Oh no."

"Hey. Don't worry. She's a nice lady."

"Pop doesn't know any nice ladies." The last girlfriend Pop brought home ended up stealing money from my soccer team and running away with it.

After I hang up, I stand there in that phone booth, and I want to punch my fist through the glass. I'm angry. I don't even know where lunch is coming from, much less dinner, much less the next day or the next. I'm tired of saying it ain't a problem he's gone. It *is* a problem. A big, big problem. Pop was *stupid* to fight in that war. *Stupid, stupid, stupid.* Now come home, Pop. Come home and buy me a lunch.

I never realized before how much care he took of me. There was always food, even if I usually had to fix it for myself. He washed laundry and worked at the quarry and did whatever he had to do to get Hoggle to let us live in the trailer. He could hit a garage sale like a whirlwind, haggle like an old gypsy, and walk away with so much clothes and junk for so little money that it was almost like a robbery.

Looks like I better get serious about taking care of myself. Or I'll end up at The Miracle Home. Or, worse yet, I'll end up nowhere. I'll starve to death.

From the trailer I fetch Pop's fishing rod. In the soft wet dirt where the washing machine drains, there are plenty of worms. Maybe I can catch a lunch.

At the lake the ducks are quacking and paddling about. I see Babcock on the far shore. I spit on the hook for luck. I cast. Reel it in. Cast again. Fishy, fishy, come bite my hook. I'll go captain, and you'll go cook.

Babcock is kneeling by the water with a big red paper cup.

It's hot, standing in the sun. I'm thirsty and getting no bites. Probably because I'm trying too hard. For fishing, you need to be patient. I ain't patient. I'm hungry. And I'm jerking the line around too much. I can't help it. I want to *do* something.

I wish I had a guitar. Or a fiddle. If you make music, the fish come to hear. And then you catch them. I wonder if Law's drums would work.

No. Drums ain't music.

Now I see Babcock standing with his arm out. I can't see that far, but I know what he's doing: moving his lips, making no sound that any person can hear. And on his finger, there'll be a big, bright dragonfly. I've seem him do it before.

After a while, Babcock with his big red paper cup walks around to where I'm standing with the fishing pole.

"Any luck?" he asks.

"Not yet," I say. "See any fish over on that side where you were?"

"Yep," Babcock says. "Big ones."

"I guess I'll try over there."

Babcock gets a worried look on his face. He says, "You planning to throw them back after you catch them?"

"No."

"Are you planning to keep them in a fish tank?"

"No, Badger. I'm gonna *eat* them."

I walk around to the other side of the lake. I stand right where Babcock was standing before. I cast.

On the other side, I see Babcock kneeling on the shore with his mouth just inches from the water.

In a half hour, I catch two duckweeds and a plastic six-pack binder. I keep searching the water, but I never see a fish, big or small.

I walk back to Babcock. I'm so thirsty I could kill.

"You lied," I say. "Ain't no fish over there."

Babcock sits back with his hands around his knees. He looks relieved. He says, "They all came over here."

I look down. Sure enough, right there at the surface is a twelve-inch bass. He looks like he's grinning. *Laughing* at me.

"They *follow* you, Badger?"

"If I call them."

"Did you call them?"

"I was talking to them."

"You *talk* to fish?"

"Sure."

"What'd they say?"

"They don't talk *words,*" Babcock says scornfully, as if anybody would know that.

"But how do you call them?"

Babcock looks at my fishing pole. He says, "I'll never tell."

"Badger, I ain't just fishing for fun. I'm fishing for *lunch.*"

"I wish *I* could have lunch," Babcock says. "A *real* lunch."

"You still drinking that diet stuff?"

"I *hate* that stuff."

I'm cooked. The sweat is pouring into my eyes so I can hardly see.

Babcock is watching a dragonfly. He wanders off, following the bright orange body.

He left his big red cup sitting on the ground. Half full.

I grab it. I toss back my head and drink it down in five big gulps. And now I see why he hates that diet stuff. It tastes awful — like dirty water with little lumps of slimy goo. I wipe my lips on the back of my hand.

Babcock wanders back.

I'm still hot, so I lie down at the edge of the pond and splash some water onto my face — dirty brown water, but at least it's cool. The water smells like Babcock's diet drink. That's what happens when you're hungry. Everything smells like food.

Babcock is standing over me. "They're *gone,*" he says.

I look up. "What's gone?"

"The dragonfly larvae. I just caught them in the pond. I had them in a red cup. And now the cup is *empty.*"

I say, "Dsh." I wonder if I'm going to throw up. Right into the pond.

"Some animal must've come along and *drank* them," Babcock says. "Now what kind of an animal would do *that?*"

"Coyote," I say.

"They wouldn't come into *town.*"

"They come right into your house and eat your food."

"I've never seen one."

"Maybe you have and didn't know it."

"You all right, Danny? You look sick."

"I think I ate too much."

"That makes me mad. That stupid animal. I'd like to get my hands on that clown."

"Be careful with clowns, Babcock."

I fished all afternoon without any bites. I wondered what I could do besides spitting on the hook to make myself lucky, and the more I thought about it, the more I realized that I'd better not wait for luck. I'll starve if I depend on luck. The longer I stood in the hot sun, the thirstier and hungrier I felt. I never had any lunch, unless you count the dragonfly larvae, and just two eggs for breakfast, and no dinner the night before, and now I needed to figure how to get dinner tonight when all I owned was two cents.

Babcock went off with his family to visit his uncle.

Well, there was one house where I knew I was always welcome: Boone's.

Flake, Boone's dog, with one ear up and one ear down, ran out and greeted me when I walked into his yard. Mrs. Barnaby opened the door with a friendly smile and said, "Hi, Danny, come on in." I walked past the kitchen with the cabinets full of food. I saw Clover unwrapping a candy bar, and I felt saliva gushing into my mouth. She said, "Hi, Danny," and I smelled chocolate on her breath, and my stomach jumped up into my throat like it was trying to grab the smell and pull it down. I was so hungry, I was shaking. I stepped on carpets that were clean in a house that never had rats under a roof that never leaked. They might not be rich. Not bankrupt rich. But they were *comfortable*. Boone was in his room, drawing a car on a drafting board that his father gave him.

I could hear Mr. Barnaby's voice in another room.

He was carrying on about something. "Right here in our town," he said. "It's happening right here under our noses."

Mrs. Barnaby said, "It's everywhere, Tom. It's worse other places. We should be thankful we're here."

He said, "I *am* thankful. But that doesn't mean I like it happening in my own town, even if it's less than elsewhere."

I heard Mrs. Barnaby say, "The sheriff will handle it."

Mr. Barnaby shouted, "The sheriff's got a whole *county* to take care of. He hasn't got time for our little town and our one little drug dealer, whoever it is."

I could tell him who it is. But that wouldn't be street. I knew when to keep my mouth shut. And anyway, some day I might need that job.

Mrs. Barnaby called out, "Time to go, everybody."

Boone set down his pencil. "Gotta go, Danny. We're going out for pizza."

Dsh. There goes dinner. If I'm at their house at mealtime, they always invite me. But going out, they don't. I don't know whether it's because they want going out to be a special time with only their family, or whether they just never think of inviting me. I ain't asking.

Coyotes don't beg. They *grab*.

Boone goes into his father's bedroom to ask him

a question. I follow. Mr. Barnaby's in the closet. On the dresser there's some keys, a pile of coins, and a fifty-dollar bill.

My belly sees that money, and it *shouts*.

"Can I get anchovies, Dad?" Boone asks.

I slip the fifty into my pocket.

Mr. Barnaby says from the closet, "You get a small pizza, and you eat *all* of it."

"I better go," I say.

"Oh. Wait," Boone says. "Danny — maybe you could have something to eat before we go."

Good old Boone. But I've got a heavy weight in my pocket, and I need to get out of the house fast before Mr. Barnaby comes out of the closet.

"Gotta go," I say.

"Bye, Danny," Mr. Barnaby calls from the closet. I never walked so fast. My heart is pounding.

"Bye, Mrs. Barnaby," I say in the kitchen.

"Bye, Danny. Want a cookie before you leave?"

"I gotta go now."

"Well. Next time. Come again."

I'm out the door and on the street.

My pocket feels like it's on fire. I break into a run.

Down by the lake, Damon Goodey's got a brand-new car: a red Pontiac Trans Am with a black flame painted on the hood.

I guess business has been good for him.

Of course, he's going to end up in jail.

Or shot dead.

Nobody would weep.

I stop in front of the grocery store. Instead of pushing the door open, I step aside and stand in front of the window with my nose against the glass. Inside I see racks of potato chips. I see a cooler full of milk and cheese. I see shelves of bread and a whole display case full of doughnuts. In the back I see the sign that says **MEATS**. By the cash register there's peanuts, candy bars, licorice. And on the floor in front of the ice-cream freezer, I see a penny.

I go inside.

I pick up the penny, go to the cash register, and buy one jawbreaker. They're one for three cents, two for a nickel. I lay my three pennies on the counter.

I walk back toward Boone's. Goodey is standing next to his new car at the lake. He's wearing a fancy silk shirt and gold chains. Smoking a cigarette. He's so dumb, he thinks smoking is cool.

Somewhere, somehow, I crossed the line. My belly was shouting so loud, it drowned out my brain. Shouting about business. Money. Food.

Well, it ain't business. It ain't grab. And it ain't street.

It's stealing.

I slip the fifty-dollar bill — with Ulysses S. Grant scowling up at me — under Boone's front door.

I suck on the jawbreaker. That's dinner.

15
THE CHASE

I was almost home in twilight trying not to think about food when on the road outside Hoggle's place I saw two gray bodies in a field among the cattle: General Mess and Miss Arool. The cows didn't pay any attention to them. But the coyotes followed the cows. Every once in a while they pounced on something, stabbing it with their forepaws, then snatching it in their teeth and shaking their heads.

Field mice.

The cows stirred up the mice when they went clomping through the grass. All the coyotes had to do was follow, and listen, and pounce. The cows helped the coyotes by finding them food, and the coyotes helped the cows by getting rid of the mice that were eating their grass. But try to explain that to a rancher.

The air was heavy and smelled like rain.

I saw a movement down the hill out of the corner of my eye: a big white dog. Whiteknight, wandering out for his nightly adventure, trotting straight up the hill like he knew exactly where he was going. The cows watched him coming every step with their big wet eyes.

The coyotes saw him, too. They were off in a flash.

Whiteknight stopped to check out a fence post. He looked up just in time to see the coyotes at the top of the hill. And he took off. He went tearing to the top of the hill and disappeared over the other side.

I hoped the coyotes had enough of a head start. I listened, but I couldn't hear anything except the moaning of a cow. I started walking to the top of the hill. When I was halfway there, all of a sudden with a thumping of feet and a whooshing through the grass here come the two coyotes with Whiteknight closing in.

The coyotes split up.

Whiteknight doesn't miss a beat — he chases General Mess. Whiteknight's bigger, stronger, maybe faster, but the General's got the advantage of knowing where he's going while Whiteknight has to react.

I watch them race up the hill again and out of sight.

I want to run up the hill and see if I can follow

where they went, but they're moving way too fast and, anyway, here comes Miss Arool. She seems to know something. She trots over to a thicket and lays down with her head up, ears erect, alert.

Nothing happens.

I bet Whiteknight can outrun General Mess. And in a fight, much as I hate to admit it, I'd bet on Whiteknight to win it. I'd like to smash that dog with a two-by-four.

Miss Arool stays alert. Her ears are like big radar dishes. They're moving slowly in a circle. I bet she can hear the chase. She knows just where they are.

She doesn't look worried.

All of a sudden here they come! General Mess comes bounding down the hill with Whiteknight barreling along behind him. The General reaches bottom and cuts to the left across the meadow right into the thicket.

And Miss Arool jumps out of the thicket. Trading places. She jumps directly in front of Whiteknight and dashes away up the hillside.

Whiteknight doesn't hesitate. He's after her.

Arool leads him under some oaks and around some rocks, then through the grass to a wire mesh fence where she scoots on her belly under the wire where there's a small opening. Whiteknight follows her to the hole, goes down on his belly, sliding forward with the momentum from his running — and yelps. He's stuck. He backs out. The wire scraped the top of his back. There's blood. But

Whiteknight doesn't stop to worry about it. He backs up on his haunches and jumps over the fence. In another moment, he's chasing Arool over the top of the hill.

They're gone.

General Mess stands there with his sides heaving for breath. His tongue hangs low, dripping. I wonder if they're going to switch off again. How much longer can Whiteknight run full tilt like that?

After General Mess catches his breath, he walks away from the thicket and across the road. I figure he knows better than I do what's going to happen next, so I follow.

The General trots to the edge of the farmyard and stops just out of the light.

I see Goldie sleeping in the dirt in front of the porch. Lights are on in Hoggle's kitchen.

Nothing happens.

I hope Miss Arool knows what she's doing. One false step — she trips — and Whiteknight can pounce on her. And if he's bigger than General Mess, he's got that much more on Arool.

The General is sniffing something on the ground. A cigarette butt. Hoggle must've thrown it there.

The General stands next to the cigarette butt, twists his body sideways, aiming, and drops down on his back on top of the butt. He wiggles, rolling, grinding the tobacco out of the butt and into his fur with his legs kicking into the air. Then he rolls back over to his feet, stands up, and shakes. Ah! Perfume!

The General's ears twitch. He's looking toward the road. I look, too.

Here comes Miss Arool. Here comes Whiteknight with his tongue dragging. Arool scoots by the pickup truck and right into the light of the farmyard — which seems crazy to me — and across toward the house and the porch. Arool leaps onto the sleeping Goldie, kicks with her hind legs, and she's off again toward the barn. Goldie jumps up with a start. Whiteknight runs into the farmyard just as Goldie is looking for something to bite — and barrels into her.

Goldie clamps her teeth onto his leg.

Whiteknight yelps. He rolls over in the dirt. He gets up and throws himself at Goldie.

It's a dogfight.

The screen door slams. Hoggle grabs a metal fence stake from a pile by the house and whales into Whiteknight.

Whiteknight lets go from the back of Goldie's neck.

Hoggle kicks him in the ribs.

Goldie crawls under the porch.

Hoggle stomps into the kitchen.

Whiteknight stands there in the farmyard, panting for breath, exhausted from the run, tricked by the coyotes, bleeding from the fence, bitten by Goldie, bruised by Hoggle, beaten, outsmarted, hurt, confused, mad.

He won't be going on any more adventuring tonight. He plops down to the ground and starts licking his leg.

General Mess is gone. So is Miss Arool. They couldn't handle Whiteknight one on one, but they could do it together.

Maybe I need a partner, too.

16
NICE MOVE

All night I dream of food. Big Al's got it all. I have to watch him as he stuffs his mouth. Every last bite of it.

I wake in a foggy gray dawn. My belly is screaming. I ransack the trailer for food. All I can find is salt, sugar, catsup, mustard, cooking oil. I pour a bowl full of sugar and spoon it into my mouth. Wash it down with a couple squirts of catsup.

Plants. Maybe I can eat plants.

Outside I find a bed of mint. Try chewing one, but it's stringy and tastes too strong, so I boil some leaves and try drinking it like tea. Not bad.

But I'm still hungry. Back outside I search around. There's dozens of different kinds of little plants. Clover. Cows like it. I try one, but it's too chewy. Berries. Yeah. Big, black, sweet, mushy berries growing in a huge tangle of thorny briars. I wade into the patch. Thorns rip at my arms and face; my hands turn purple; a blue jay scolds. I pluck berries and stuff them into my mouth until my arms are bleeding from gashes.

That's better.

Now I was ready to face Hoggle. I walked up to his house, knocked on his door.

"Mr. Hoggle, I wondered if I could make a deal."

"A deal? What happened to you, Danny? You look like you got in a fight with a Purple People Eater. And lost."

"I picked some berries. The deal is, I'd like to have the job of collecting your eggs every morning. And the pay is, I get to keep two eggs."

"Hm. You've already been collecting them, Danny. Did you by any chance happen to hold on to some of those eggs?"

"It just might have happened."

"So now you want to make it a permanent arrangement?"

"I want to make it honest. I want to make it suit my business philosophy."

"Which is?"

"Don't steal."

"Hm," Hoggle said. He gave me a look like he was wondering, Where did I go wrong in teaching this boy? Then he said, "Well, Danny, I tell you what. How about if you feed the chickens, too? And how about if you're responsible for making sure the fence is in repair and keeping the water topped up and cleaning out the guano? And you can make sure they aren't pecking each other to death, and check to see if they've got any diseases. And for that, you leave two eggs on my doorstep and keep all the rest for yourself. Would that suit your philosophy?"

"Yes, sir."

"Then it's a deal. And how would you like a big white worthless dog, too?"

"Uh, no. I already got — I mean, uh, no thank you."

"Smart. Very smart, Danny. And you're smart to be so young. Stupidest thing I ever did was to go and get old. Don't ever do it, Danny. Too much work to keep this place up. Ought to give up tractor work, too, except the money's so good. But the animals aren't worth it. Look at Burke. He's lost three sheep. Coyotes are running them down. He's fit to be tied."

"What's he going to do about the — uh — coyote problem?"

"More poison. Set traps. Hunt. Shoot."

I wished I had a gun I could give to the coyotes. So they could shoot back.

I knew I'd better change the subject, or I'd give them away.

"Uh — Mr. Hoggle?"

"What, Danny?"

"What's going to happen with that swimming pool?"

"They called me today. They want to go ahead with it. They promised that their son and his fat little lawyer wouldn't give me any more trouble. But they want me to get a permit. Rich people, you know — them Livermore people — want to do it by the book. The trouble is, to get a permit, I have to get a sign-off by a geologist."

"What's a sign-off?"

"It means you hire a geologist, and you wait a few weeks, and he never shows up, and you wait a few more weeks, and you call him and chew him out, and you wait a few more weeks, and he comes out and walks over the land, and then he goes back to his office, and you wait a few weeks, and you call him and chew him out, and you wait a few more weeks, and he writes a report, and you pay him a thousand dollars. And then you go ahead and do what you were planning to do anyway."

"Do you have a geologist?"

"You're looking at him." He grinned.

"If you're a geologist, I'm a new clear fist."

"I've got a geology report from a different job I did a long time ago. I'll just copy it. And sign it. And charge Mr. Livermore a thousand dollars for it. That's good business, Danny. And that's *my* philosophy."

"I'll get your eggs, Mr. Hoggle."

"Good deal."

I found six eggs. I gave Mr. Hoggle his two, took the other four home, scrambled them, and ate. Then I was off to school.

Boone met me in the schoolyard and told me his father lost fifty dollars last night and was blaming me for it. Boone said, "He was ranting and raving and saying he'd never trust you again, Danny. He called you a juvenile delinquint. Then when he came home, my father found the money on the floor. He must have dropped it there."

"Is he still mad?"

"No. Now he feels guilty for saying all those awful things about you."

"Tell him not to feel guilty," I said. "He changed his mind — that's all. Sometimes I change my mind, too."

After school I stayed for soccer practice with the Noodledoods. Walt changed the day for Slime practice so we could do both. Which seemed like a dirty trick to Babcock because he was hoping to get out of running laps for the rest of the season.

The first thing Mr. Barnaby did was tell the Noodledoods that the best way to begin a practice is to run a lap. "You big boys," Mr. Barnaby said, "you run with the team. To set the pace."

Babcock rolled his eyes.

So we ran once around the field — Geraldine in front, then Boone and me, then little Brian, then a big pack of Noodledoods, then Dylan, then Babcock. Geraldine could run forever. She's got legs like a deer. Brian, her brother, was right on our heels, which was surprising for a little kid whose legs hadn't sprouted out yet. He runs on determination. The opposite of Dylan. Not that Dylan's slow — it's just that he forgets. His mind wanders, and he slows down, and he reaches out to catch a grasshopper, and unless somebody yells at him, he's likely to never come back. Babcock, now, Babcock is slow — over long distances. Put him in a goal, though, and he can explode.

Mr. Barnaby broke us up into groups. Babcock would teach a goalie clinic. Dylan and Boone would teach defense. Geraldine and I would teach offense.

"Wait," Dylan said. "Could I teach offense?"

I knew why. He wanted to be with Geraldine.

"I suppose so," Mr. Barnaby said.

Dylan smiled.

"Okay," Mr. Barnaby said. "Geraldine, you go teach defense with Boone. Dylan and Danny will teach offense."

Dylan frowned. He said, "Wait. Could you let Danny do defense?"

"I suppose," Mr. Barnaby said.

Dylan smiled.

"Danny," Mr. Barnaby said, "you go join Geraldine with defense. Boone and Dylan can teach offense."

"No. Wait," Dylan said. He looked like he'd swallowed a fly. He said, "I mean . . . I wanted . . . let

Geraldine do offense. And Boone do defense. And — "

"Dylan," Mr. Barnaby said, "I'm trying to please you, but you keep changing your mind. Now we've got a practice to run here. I guess we'll just do it my way. Danny and Geraldine, offense. Boone and Dylan, defense."

Then Mr. Barnaby divided the Noodledoods into groups that would rotate through our clinics.

There were four kids in our group. Geraldine took two and taught them how to dribble. I took the other two and tried to teach passing. Mr. Barnaby stayed with me. I bet he remembered what I said at dinner the other night about how he needed to be tougher on these kids, and he wanted to keep an eye on me.

My two kids were Clover and Brian. I set up a passing drill where they were supposed to pass back and forth as they ran down the field. First Clover, with her pink shoelaces and a pink bow in her hair, little Clover tapped a pass to Brian and started running forward. Brian stepped up to the ball — and *creamed* it. The ball blasted into Clover's stomach. She fell backward and lay there on the ground looking up at the sky.

"Nice stop, Clover," Mr. Barnaby said.

"Huh?" Clover said.

"That's the way to use your body to stop the ball," Mr. Barnaby said.

"Oh. Yeah," Clover said. She got up.

"That was a good strong kick, Brian," Mr. Barnaby said.

"Yep." Brian smiled.

"Next time, let's try to place it a little in front of her so she can run up to it. And soft, so it won't go too far. I know you can do that, Brian, because you're my best kicker."

"Yep," Brian said.

Brian thought Mr. Barnaby paid him a compliment. He *did* pay him a compliment. But he also told Brian that he'd done it all wrong, and somehow Mr. Barnaby made it sound like praise.

Brian tried again. He kicked a little roller right in front of Clover.

"Great pass!" Mr. Barnaby shouted.

Clover ran forward toward the ball — and stepped in a gopher hole. She fell forward, did two forward rolls, and stopped with her head between her feet.

"You all right?" Mr. Barnaby asked.

"I think so," Clover said.

"Those were good forward rolls," Mr. Barnaby said. "I'm glad you know how to make a soft landing."

I was getting the hang of it, this positive coaching.

With the next two kids, Mr. Barnaby stepped back and let me handle it. A boy and a girl. I got them started. The girl ran up to the ball and kicked it — exactly opposite from where her passing partner was standing.

"Uh — good kick," I said. "That's putting your foot on it."

She fetched the ball and tried again. This time the ball went where she wanted it — right in front of the boy.

"Nice pass," I said.

The boy ran to the ball, swung his foot for a kick, and missed completely as the ball rolled by.

"Uh — um — good approach," I said. "That's the way to come up on the ball."

The boy tried again. He fetched the ball and kicked it way downfield.

"That's leading her," I said. "That's the idea."

I could do it. It felt like lying, but I could do it. It didn't seem honest to praise somebody for some little thing when the fact is they *blew* it on the big thing. But it worked. They kept trying. I kept praising. And they got better. They actually were improving right before my eyes. Sometimes I had to reach way out for a compliment — like, those sure are nice-looking shoes you got there — but I found something to say.

So it worked. The Noodledoods weren't ready for the pros yet, but they were a better team. And I was glad.

One thing, though, made me sad. This coaching — this positive attitude — it would be nice to be on the receiving end some time. Just once I want to hear somebody say, "Nice move, Danny. Never mind that your father's gone, and all your plans for

business seem to go up in smoke, and you've got
to scuffle for food, and you're scared to even dream,
and nobody cares for you any more than a rancher
cares for a coyote — never mind all that, Danny.
Nice move. Nice move, Danny. Nice move."

After dinner at Boone's in their house under the
redwood trees, I helped clear the table. I always
cleared my own plate, but now I'm thinking I ought
to help more. After all, I ain't paying for all this
food. And I never feed Boone at my house. He never
comes to my trailer since we moved out of town.
Nobody does.

In the kitchen I got an idea. I said to Mrs. Barnaby,
"Those are mighty fine muffins you make."

"Why, thank you, Danny." She looked pleased.

"Mrs. Barnaby, I was wondering, would you like
some eggs?"

"What kind of eggs?"

"Fresh eggs. You see, I'm in charge of Mr. Hoggle's chickens now, and I'm gonna end up with more
eggs than I — I mean, we — you know, my father
and me — more than we can eat. So I was wondering if you'd like some. I could probably get you
a dozen every week."

"Fresh eggs? I'd love them. That would be wonderful, Danny. I tell you what. Would you and your
father like some muffins? We could do a trade."

Exactly what I had in mind. "He'd like that," I
said. "He likes homecooked muffins."

"You should bring him here for dinner some time."

"He's real busy. I don't think — "

"Busy? What's he doing?"

"He — uh — he's been doing some stuff at the VA hospital."

"Oh, really? You mean he's a volunteer?"

"Yeah. I guess you could say that."

"That must be very rewarding."

"I — uh — I hope so."

While running home, by the lake I saw Damon Goodey and his red Trans Am, Goodey with a big flashy ring on his finger and hair hanging in his face. Goodey, getting more money faster than anybody else in this town.

The coyotes weren't around when I came home. I hoped they weren't chasing sheep. I went to bed and fell into a dream, and suddenly there was a coyote riot going on. There was screeching and wailing and barking like fifteen coyotes gone berserk, like a whole pack of coyotes was attacking some animal — maybe they were ganging up on a *cow*.

I jumped up from bed and looked out the window.

And there's Miss Arool. General Mess. Sitting on their haunches, singing a duet. Just them. Just singing. Throwing their voices so each of them sounds like half a dozen different animals.

I guess it's coyote rock-and-roll.

I go back to bed. It's nice to have food in my belly. It's nice to have coyote music in my ears. I know what they're singing. They're saying, "You made two good deals today, Danny. Honest deals. You're getting eggs from Hoggle and muffins from Mrs. Barnaby. Nice move. Nice move, Danny. Nice move."

17
THE DEAL

It was a misty, foggy, gray morning. I collected eight eggs from the chickens, left two for Hoggle, went back to the trailer and turned on the stove.

Nothing happened.

I went outside and checked the dial on the propane tank. Empty.

So much for cooking. Did I want to eat six raw eggs? No, thank you. It's time to hustle.

I put the eggs in a paper bag and run to Boone's house — and on the way, under a tree at the side of the road, somebody's dumped a mattress, a couple garbage bags, and — a treasure! — a bicycle frame. Rusty, but it ain't bent. Now all I need is a pair of pedals.

I give Mrs. Barnaby the half dozen eggs. She's

surprised to see me so early, and she says she doesn't have the muffins made yet for trade, but she invites me in for orange juice and cereal. Which is fine with me. Then before it's time for Boone to leave for school, I run back and get the bicycle frame and take it home.

At school I tell Boone I'm building a bicycle, and all I need is a pair of pedals. "You got any, Boone?"

"No. Sorry."

Neither does Geraldine. Or Dylan. But Babcock does.

"Can I have them, Babcock?"

"What'll you give me?"

"Why do I have to give you anything? What are you going to do with an extra pair of bicycle pedals?"

"I might need them some day."

"If you need them some day, I'll give them *back*."

"No. You might wreck them. Or lose them. What'll you give me?"

"What do you want?"

"A hamster."

"A hamster! Badger, I don't have a hamster."

Babcock folds his arms across his chest. "That's what I want," he says.

I see there's no arguing. So I start asking around to see if anybody has a hamster. I ask all the seventh grade, then all the sixth grade, then I start on the fifth grade and come upon Davey.

"I got a horned toad," Davey says.

"I don't need a horny toad," I say. "I need a hamster."

"Horned toad's just as good."

"I don't think so. But, just in case — would you trade him?"

"What'll you give me?"

"What do you want?"

"A baseball bat."

I don't have a baseball bat. And I don't want a horny toad. But maybe there's a way to work something out here. I start asking if anybody wants to trade a baseball bat. I find a sixth-grader named Mike who has two baseball bats that are too small for him.

"Will you trade them?" I ask.

"What'll you give me?"

"What do you want?"

"I don't know." He shrugs. "Nothing."

"You must want *something*."

"You know what? I always wanted an ant farm."

"An ant farm? I don't have an ant farm."

But I ask around. And sure enough, Boone says his little sister, Clover, has an ant farm. Except the ants all died.

"Clover," I say, "would you trade your ant farm for something?"

"For what?"

"A baseball bat." Because Mike will give me two bats, and Davey only asked for one, so I've got one left over.

"No," Clover says, "I don't want a baseball bat."

"What do you want?"

She thinks a minute. Then she says, "I want a purple pony."

"But, Clover, ponies aren't purple."

"Not a *real* pony."

So I ask around. Mary Lynn's got a purple unicorn, not a pony, and she'd be willing to trade for a jump rope because her brother used her old jump rope to tie up the dog, and the dog chewed a hole in it. And Brian's got a brand-new jump rope somebody gave him for his birthday, but he doesn't want it because he thinks jump ropes are for girls, and of course he's wrong but I don't tell him, and what he wants for his jump rope is a copy of *Mad* magazine, the one from a few months ago where they show a football game played by gorillas. And little José's got thirteen *Mad* magazines, including the one with the football game, and he says he'll give them to me for nothing because he doesn't want them anymore, and I say "I'll give you a baseball bat for them anyway," and he gets this big grin and says, "Okay! Okeedokee!"

I tell José to bring the *Mads* tomorrow, and he should give the football one to Brian and the rest to me. Next I tell Brian that José will bring him the *Mad*, and he should bring his jump rope to school and give it to Mary Lynn. I tell Mary Lynn that Brian will give her a jump rope, and she should bring her purple unicorn and give it to Clover. Then I tell

Clover that I couldn't find a purple pony, but I found a purple unicorn and would that be all right?

She thinks a minute. She says, "Do unicorns like cats?"

"Oh yes," I say. "Unicorns *love* cats."

"Okay," she says.

So I tell Clover that Mary Lynn will bring her a purple unicorn, and she should bring her ant farm and give it to Mike. Then I find Mike and tell him that Clover will bring him an ant farm, except the ants all died but he can find some more, and he should bring his baseball bats and give one to Davey and the other to little José. Then I tell Davey that Mike will bring you a baseball bat that's too small for him but should be just right for you because you're shorter, and you should bring your horny toad and give it to Babcock.

"Babcock," I say, "I think we got a deal."

"You found a hamster?"

"Not exactly. But I found something just as good."

"A guinea pig?"

"Well, no, but — "

"A white mouse?"

"No. A horny toad."

For a good five seconds, Babcock doesn't say anything. He just looks at me through those thick eyeglasses, and I can't tell whether I have a deal or just a house of cards. One word, and he could blow it all down.

Babcock sighs. He says, "I still want a hamster."

"Aaaa-aagh!"

"But I'd like a horned toad, too."

I look closely at Babcock. Is he hosing me, too? I say, "Then it's a deal?"

"Deal. And Danny . . ."

"What?"

Babcock smiles. "Congratulations."

"For what?"

"For being Danny."

Then I smile, too. I say, "Just call me Danny Deal."

18
HELPING DYLAN

Law came to soccer practice on Tuesday, just as he'd promised. He was already a lot better, just from the practice he'd had with me in his yard. Plus he'd been practicing by himself, he said, kicking a ball against the garage door until his mother told him to stop because it made scuff marks on the paint.

At the end of practice, Walt warned us about our next game.

"This team wasn't in our league last year. They're not from Pulgas Park."

"Where are they from?" I asked.

"Piojo Grande."

That's the town right next to Pulgas Park.

Geraldine asked, "Why didn't they stay in their old league in Piojo Grande?"

"They were expelled," Walt said.

"What for?" Geraldine asked.

"Hacking. Tripping. Fighting. Cheating. Using phony birth certificates. Slashing the ref's tires."

Geraldine's eyes lit up. "They really did that?" she said.

Babcock said, "So what are they doing in *our* league?"

"The coach promised to clean up his act."

"Did he?"

"Well, last week I scouted their game. And no, they haven't changed. Not very much."

"They were playing dirty?"

"Tripping. Hacking. Bad-mouthing. Intimidation."

"Wow," Geraldine said. "Why can't *we* be like that?"

"Because we're better than that. That kind of poor sportsmanship would be beneath our dignity," Walt said with a rueful smile, "the dignity of the Sucking Slime."

"Forget dignity," Geraldine said. "Let's win."

"Let's set a more modest goal," Walt said. "This team won its last game twenty-two to nothing. Last year no team ever came within ten points of them. The shortest player on their team is six inches taller than you, Geraldine, even including your hair. And you're our tallest player."

Boone spoke up. "What we need," he said, "is a positive attitude."

"Yeah," Babcock said. "Why don't we just forfeit? That way we could stay home and do something useful. That would be positive."

"No," Boone said. "A forfeit isn't positive."

"What is?" Babcock asked. "Getting stomped?"

"Victory," Boone said.

"Oh, sure," Babcock said, looking disgusted.

"You've got to have a positive attitude," Boone said. "It might feel like a victory if we could hold them to less than ten points. It might feel like a victory if we could score just once. And it might be a victory if we could come out of this game feeling good about ourselves. Because we played right. Played *fair*. And it would help if we had lots of people on the sidelines cheering for us. Cheering with a positive attitude."

"Where do we get all these people?" Babcock said.

"Your parents. Your friends. Your brothers and sisters. And the Noodledood parents. Their game is just before ours. They can stay and watch. I'll ask my father to ask them."

"Sounds good to me, Boone," Walt said.

"If somebody hacks me," Geraldine said, "I'm hacking them back."

"You do, and you're out of the game," Walt said.

"That might be a blessing," Babcock said.

"Babcock. Think positive," Walt said.

"Yes, sir. I am positively thinking. I positively think playing goalie against this team will be like standing in front of a machine gun."

"We'll be cheering for you, Babcock."

"Yes, sir."

Dylan came up to me after practice. "Can you help me?" he said. "I've got a problem with Geraldine."

"What's the problem?"

"I want to ask her out."

"So what's the problem?"

"I can't do it."

"Well, sure, you can't drive a car, but there oughta be some way — "

"Not that," Dylan said. "I could get a ride or something. The problem is, I can't ask her."

"Says who?"

"Nobody."

"Then who's stopping you from asking her?"

"Nobody."

"So ask her."

"I can't."

"Why not?"

"Because she might say no."

Dylan took the comb out of his back pocket and touched up his hair.

If you asked me, Geraldine would be doing him a favor if she said no. Then he wouldn't have to spend any money or get dressed up or make any arrangements just so he could take her somewhere and — and do what? Whatever people do when they go out. Be with her. Talk to her. You can talk to Geraldine any time you want. You just sit down next to her and start talking. But I guess Dylan wanted to make it a big deal.

"Dylan, what you need is a more positive attitude."

"Just help."

"So what do you want me to do?" I said.

"Ask her," Dylan said. "For me."

"You want *me* to ask her if she'll go on a date with *you*?"

"Right. Except, don't call it a date."

"Why not?"

"It sounds so *formal*. I just want to go out with her."

"Then *tell* her."

"I can't. You tell her."

"But why, Dylan? She still might say no."

"But then she wouldn't say it to me."

"But she'd say it to me, and I'd say it to you."

"That's okay. And also, she might say yes."

"She might say yes if you asked her yourself."

"But she might also say no."

"But — Dylan — it don't make no difference."

"Just do it, Danny. As a favor. Please."

We walked to Dylan's house. I figured at least I'd get dinner for my trouble.

The phone was in the kitchen. Dylan dialed. He knew the number from memory, even though he'd never called her. He'd probably been thinking about it for weeks. I bet he dialed the number and then hung up before it could ring.

I bet he was in hell.

I heard it ring once, twice, three times.

"Hello?" A woman's voice.

"Could I speak to Geraldine, please?"

"Who's calling?"

"This is Danny."

I could hear the phone clunk down on the tabletop or something.

I had no idea what I was going to say.

"Hello? Danny?" It was Geraldine.

"Hi, Geraldine. This is Danny."

"I know."

"Oh. Good. Hey. Listen. How ya doing?"

"Fine."

"Good. Well. Hm. Was that a good soccer practice today?"

"I suppose."

"Good. Yeah. Uh. Look. The reason I'm calling is, I was wondering if you could go on a — I mean, go out with somebody. You see, I'm — "

"Sure, Danny. I'd be glad to go out with you."

"No no. You see, I'm over at Dylan's house. This is Dylan's phone."

"Where do you want to go, Danny?"

"That ain't it, Geraldine. You see, it ain't me. It's — "

"We could do something after the soccer game next Saturday. That way we'll already be in town,

and all we have to do is arrange for a ride home.
I bet my mom would pick us up."

"You up. She'd pick *you* up."

"Don't you want a ride home, too?"

"It ain't me, Geraldine. It's Dylan. Dylan needs a
ride home."

"What's Dylan going to be doing there?"

"On a *date*, Geraldine. Oops. I mean, not a date,
but he wants to go out."

"So he needs a ride home? That's okay. My mom
can give us all a ride."

"With *you*, Geraldine."

"Who's Dylan going out with?"

"You."

"You and me, and Dylan and who else?"

"Nobody else. Just Dylan. Just you."

"That's silly — you and me and Dylan."

"No. Not me."

"Danny. Is this a joke?"

"No."

"Is this serious? I mean, did you call to arrange
a date, or what?"

"No. Not a date. I called to ask you to go out.
But — "

"Then let's do it. Forget Dylan. I don't want him
tagging along. He's such a *creep*."

"No he ain't."

"He's always hanging around. Combing his hair.
You don't see me combing *my* hair all the time, do
you?"

If you wanted to comb Geraldine's hair, you'd have to use a rake. But I don't say so.

"Well this is great, Danny. I'm glad you called. I'll see you after the game."

"But wait. Geraldine. I can't do it."

"Why not?"

"I — um — I didn't plan on this."

"Well, you called me, didn't you?"

"Yeah, but — "

"Then what's the matter?"

"It wasn't supposed to come out this way."

"You mean this is all a *prank*?"

"No."

"If this is a joke, Danny, you're gonna be wearing my cleats in your face."

"It ain't a joke. It's just — I don't know what to do now."

"What's the matter?"

"First of all, I got no money."

"No problem. I'll pay."

"Second of all I wasn't even supposed to — "

"Oh. Excuse me. My mom needs to use the phone. Bye, Danny."

"Wait! Geraldine!"

Click.

I hung up the phone and glanced over to see Dylan sitting on a bar stool, and I knew from the look on his face that I wasn't staying for dinner, not today, and not for a long time to come.

19
LIVING THIN

The next morning I brought eggs to Mrs. Barnaby. She said my muffins were cooking in the oven. Would I like to come in and have breakfast?

"Well," I said, "I suppose I could have a little."

I ate five bowls of cornflakes, two glasses of milk, and four strips of bacon. Clover said, "Danny, you eat like a garbage disposer."

Mr. Barnaby said, "The boy has a healthy appetite."

"You'll get *fat*," Clover said.

"Do I look fat?" I said.

Mrs. Barnaby frowned. "You look thinner than I've ever seen you, Danny. Are you all right?"

"I'm fine."

"Is everything all right at home?"

"Everything's fine," I said a little too loud.

Mrs. Barnaby looked at Mr. Barnaby. But they didn't say anything more about it.

Before school, Babcock gave me the bicycle pedals. Davey gave Babcock the horny toad, which Babcock put in his pocket. Mike gave Davey one of the baseball bats, the bigger one, which had some pocks in it where he was hitting rocks, but Davey said it was okay. Clover gave Mike the ant farm and told him to be sure to catch all his ants from the same colony or there'd be a war. Mary Lynn gave Clover the purple unicorn, which was missing one eye but Clover said she'd make an eye patch for it. Brian gave Mary Lynn the jump rope, and Mike gave little José the other baseball bat, which was hardly more than a toothpick but just right for José, and José gave me thirteen *Mad* magazines, and I gave Brian the *Mad* magazine that showed the football game with the gorillas.

"Wait a minute," Brian said.

"What's the matter?"

"The cover's torn."

"So? It's all there. It's just got a tear in it."

"I want it untorn. Or else I want my jump rope back."

Dsh. If he took the jump rope back, the whole deal unraveled like a sweater caught on a snag.

"Brian," I said, "we made a deal."

"You didn't tell me it was *ripped*."

"It ain't ripped. It's *torn*."

"Torn *schmorn*. I want my jump rope back."

Brian looked at me like I was a fullback standing between him and the goal. And he just might mow me down.

I usually play forward, but I know some defense moves, too.

"Okay, Brian," I said. "You tell Mary Lynn she can't have a jump rope, which she's jumping with right now, and you tell Clover she can't have the unicorn she wants to make the eye patch for. Tell Mike he can't keep the ant farm that he's already catching ants for, tell Davey he can't have a base-ball bat, and tell little José he can't keep the base-ball bat, which he's standing there grinning about. And then tell Babcock he can't have a horny toad, which he's petting in his pocket. Go ahead, Brian. Tell them they can't have what they want because the cover's torn on your magazine."

Brian ran his eyes around at all the other faces. Little José looked worried. Davey looked angry. Clover looked sad. Babcock looked determined. Mike looked nervous. Mary Lynn looked puzzled. Then Brian turned his eyes back to me.

"I can't," he said.

Everybody let out a sigh of relief. Especially me. Clover hugged her unicorn. Davey swung his bat.

"Okay!" little José said. "Okeedokee!"

"But if you ever do this again," Brian said, "I'll

tell my big sister on you. And she'll beat you up."

Knowing Geraldine, I believe she would.

I walked home carrying twelve muffins from Mrs. Barnaby, twelve *Mads* from little José, and the pair of bicycle pedals from Babcock.

At the trailer I pulled out Pop's toolbox and set to work. I attached the smaller tire, which was the fat type, to the front of the frame. For the rear wheel I used a bigger one, a thin tire that must've come from an old three-speed bike because it had a little chain sticking out that you're supposed to attach the gear cable to. I had no gear cable, so it'd just be one speed for me: high gear. It had a coaster brake, though, so at least I could stop.

I screwed in the pedals, and I had me a bike. It looked a little funny with a small fat front wheel and a big thin rear, and when I sat on the seat I felt like I was falling forward, but when I pushed the pedals, *it moved!* Then I tried the brakes. They groaned like an old garbage truck, but they stopped the bike.

So I went for a ride.

First place I went was to the top of the driveway and Hoggle's farmyard, where he was putting some food out for Goldie on the porch. Hoggle saw me and said, "You seen Whiteknight, Danny? He went out wandering last night, and he never came back."

"No," I said. "Not today."

Hoggle looked my bike up and down. He said, "Where'd you get that old jalopy?"

"Made it."

"Where'd you get the parts?"

"Found 'em."

"That's the best way, Danny. Why buy it if you can build it? And as for parts, there's so much garbage in this world — whatever you need, it's out there somewhere. You can't beat the price."

"That's what I say, Mr. Hoggle. That's my philosophy."

"Mine, too."

It puzzled me some to be agreeing with Hoggle on a matter of business philosophy, but before I could ponder it, a beat-up old pickup truck came rattlebanging into the yard, and Burke, the sheep farmer from up the road, climbed out. He was wearing blue overalls and a hat like a baseball cap, except it had the name of a seed company on it, and he walked up to Hoggle without a greeting and without a smile. Real solemn, he said, "Henry, I shot the varmint that was running down my sheep."

I felt a chill.

"Good, Abner, good for you," Hoggle said.

I was thinking: He said varmint. Only one.

I wanted to run away. Ride away. Forever. But I couldn't move.

Burke said, "I brought him for you to see, Henry."

"Why, Abner?"

Burke walked over to the rear of the truck and dropped the tailgate. And there, laying on his side with his mouth hanging open and his teeth looking ready to bite, his four legs out straight like he was caught running and never would stop, there was the body — of a big, white, dead dog. Whiteknight.

"Because he's yours," Burke said.

"Abner, I'm sorry," Hoggle said. "I should've known."

"We all should've known," Burke said.

In the mailbox mixed in with all the junk, I found a postcard. Right away I recognized Pop's jaggedy handwriting:

> *Dear Danny,*
>   *Tommy says you're okay. That's good.*
> *I'm okay, too. Who are you staying*
> *with? Boone? I'll be home soon. I'm*
> *sorry about the television. I got a friend.*
> *She got to move. You know how that is.*
> *She got no place to go.*
>
>   *Pop*

At the bottom he wrote an address, but no phone number.

Dsh, I'm thinking. *That* kind of friend.

But I'm glad he's okay.

*   *   *

I rode my bike to town — to the grocery store — and parked next to a couple of eighteen-speed racing bikes with sparkly paint. Two guys were standing next to the bikes wearing some Martian-type clothing, glowing and skintight, with white helmets and wraparound sunglasses.

My brakes groaned when I stopped.

I started to walk into the store.

"Aren't you going to lock your bike?" one of the Martians asked, teasing. "Somebody might steal it."

Then both the Martians laughed.

I found Kim, the Korean who owns the store, slicing salami behind the meat counter. He peered over the scale and said, "Can I help you?"

"I'm looking for a job," I said. "You got any work I can do? You want me to pile up some cans?"

Kim shook his head. "No can do," he said. "I got the family."

His wife and two kids all worked at the store. They came from over the hill at six in the morning and stayed until ten at night, then drove away in a Chevy station wagon that looks so old, it probably came over the desert with a wagon train. It's got holes in the sides, like Indians were shooting at it.

I tried the post office.

I told the woman at the window that I was looking for a job.

"How old are you?" she said.

"Sixteen," I said. What a lie.

She blinked.

"I'm short," I said. No lie, there.

She handed me a clipboard with three pages on it. "Fill out the application," she said. "Don't leave any blanks. Then they'll schedule you for an examination. Then, based on the results of the examination, they may call you for an interview."

"When?"

"The next exam's in about three weeks."

"I need a job now."

"Sorry."

I looked at the application. First thing it wants is my Social Security number. Then my driver's license number. Then my phone number.

That's three blanks, right there.

"Never mind," I said. "Thanks, anyway."

I rode over to the restaurant.

Inside, a man with a big droopy mustache was spinning pizza dough on his fingers.

"Hey," I said, "if I want a job here, do I gotta fill out an application for three pages and don't leave any blanks?"

He shook his head, watching the pizza spinning on his fingertips. "No," he said.

"Do I gotta take an exam and then get called in for an interview?"

"No."

"Great. Well, here I am. What should I do for you?"

He set the dough down on a tray. "Buy a hundred pizzas," he said. "Then I'd have enough business that I'd need to hire somebody."

"You don't need me?"

He shook his head. "There's no money in this town."

Riding back by the store, I saw Kim outside with his head under the hood of the old Chevy station wagon. So I stopped and asked him, "What's the matter with the car?"

"Dunno," he said.

I stuck my head under the hood with his. Probably an arrowhead stuck in the carburetor.

"Won't start?" I asked.

"Stupid car," he said.

I pulled out the dipstick. The oil was a quart low — and black as coal. "Needs oil," I said. "In fact, it needs a whole oil change."

"Yes." Kim sighed. "But that's not the problem."

"I just thought you might want to know."

"Thank you."

I unscrewed the radiator cap and looked inside. "Needs water," I said. "Lemme fill it for you."

"Thank you," Kim said. "But that's not the problem."

I found a paper cup in a garbage can and filled it with water from a hose outlet at the back of the store, then poured the water into the radiator. It took four cups.

Kim was still leaning over the engine, resting on his arms, not fiddling with anything, just staring.

I opened the battery caps and looked inside. They were okay. I pushed my thumb against the fan belt, and it gave a little, not much. I jiggled a couple of hose connections. Then I pinched the ends of the spark plug wires where they connected to the distributor cap.

"What are you doing?" Kim said.

"Nothing," I said.

When he looked at an engine, he *looked*. I touched.

"What happens when you try to start?" I asked.

"It won't catch."

"Can I try?"

Kim looked at me. "You ever drive a car?" he said.

"Once. In a driveway."

"Go ahead."

I sat down behind the wheel. The seatcover was worn off, so he'd covered it with a wicker mat. The gear was in Park. I turned the key.

Har-rump. Har-rump.

I let go of the key and leaned my head out the window.

"Is that what it did for you?"

"Yes."

I turned the key again.

Har-rump. Har-rump. Har-*rooooom*.

I tapped the gas. *Roooooom*.

Black smoke poured out from the rear.

Kim was smiling. "How'd you start it?" he asked.

"Musta been a loose wire from the spark plug," I said.

"If you need a job, Danny, you should work in a gas station."

"Ain't no gas station in San Puerco. Anyway, they wouldn't hire me. I'm too young. Nobody's gonna give me a job."

"Thanks for fixing the car." Kim reached inside and turned off the key.

"You should change that oil soon," I said.

"I don't have time. I'm here at the store all day. Where can I find a mechanic who works before six in the morning or after ten at night?"

"You could do it yourself."

"You do that?"

"That's right. Even I can do it."

"You do it for me? I pay you."

So all of a sudden, I had a job.

Kim had oil for sale in the store but no filters, so I had to skip that part. I rode home and got a wrench from Pop's toolbox, then rode back to the store and drained the oil into a big old empty fruit salad can. I remembered to replace the drain plug, then poured in the oil. Nothing to it, except my hands and arms turned black up to the elbows.

"There's a sink in the back of the store," Kim said. "You can wash up. And here." He opened the cash register and took out a five-dollar bill. "This is for you."

I washed up. Then with the five dollars I bought a half gallon of milk, a loaf of bread, and a jar of peanut butter.

And I'm wondering, who else in town needs an oil change?

20
A Nose on the Knee

Next day after school I hopped on my bike with a couple of wrenches and headed for town. The first two doors I knocked on, nobody answered. At the third house there was a brown Toyota, dirty but new-looking. A woman opened the door holding a baby in her arms. I asked her if I could change the oil in her car.

She laughed.

"What's so funny?" I asked.

"I'm sorry," she said. "I always take my car to the dealer for service. Because I want it done right. I wouldn't trust a gas station. And here I'd be trusting it to a *child* . . ."

I felt my face getting hot. I wanted to shout at her *I ain't no child and I can change your oil just as good as they can,* but I caught myself and a good thing, too, because the fact is, she's right, that is, technically, I *am* a child. And anyway, the next thing she said was:

"I just had the car serviced a couple of weeks ago. So, you see . . ."

"Okay," I said, "sorry to bother you. I just thought it looked like it might need it, being so dirty and all."

"That's okay." She shifted the baby in her arms. "Dsh."

"I beg your pardon?"

"I was just wondering, could I wash the car for you? Or if you got some wax, I could do that, too."

"Hey. Now you're talking."

In her garage she had a bucket and a sponge and some wax. And I had a job.

When I finished her car, I tried hosing and waxing my bike, but it didn't help the looks much.

I tried some more houses. Nobody wanted an oil change. But I found someone who wanted a heap of firewood stacked into a pile and another person who wanted me to pull up all the ivy growing on the ground and climbing up the trunks of her trees. And then she wants me to pull up the blackberry brambles and the Scotch broom and — hey, not that, that's fuchsia, don't you know the difference between Scotch broom and fuchsia? Well, I didn't, but I learned.

I rode the jalopybike home with a pocketful of dollar bills. For dinner, I fixed a peanut butter triple-decker sandwich, washed it down with a cup of milk, and went out to pick blackberries for dessert.

I was wearing shorts because all my pants were dirty. The blackberry thorns grabbed at my legs, so I tried to stand back and lean forward.

Something cold and wet pressed into the back of my knee.

A coyote nose. Miss Arool.

I freeze. She's the shy one. She's never been this close. She looks up at me, gives a little whine, then turns and trots away.

I haven't seen the coyotes for a couple of days. I've been worried.

After she trots about twenty feet from me, she stops and looks back.

I unfreeze, take a step toward her. She trots on. I follow. She checks every now and then to make sure I'm still coming. She leads me up the trail along the fence line where I saw the General do his clown act before. We come to the corner of the field and slip through some barbed wire and follow another trail along another fence line to a gully where you need to jump about two feet across — and here Miss Arool stops. What is she doing? She steps to the side, and then jumps. I wonder: Why the side-step? Why didn't she just keep going straight ahead? The gully's no different where she jumped.

Then I see.

There's a trap. Somebody — Burke, I guess, because this is his land — set a trap on the trail right where a coyote would jump into it when he crosses the gully. Pop told me coyotes always follow the same trails, so if you know where they go, you can just leave a trap and they'll walk right into it.

The trap is sprung. But there's no animal caught in it. Just a little clump of fur. Gray fur. Bloody. A stump. A stump of a leg, and a paw. And a mess of flies.

I follow Arool. She's left the trail and is walking up the gully around some scrawny bushes to where there's some rocks, and under the overhang of one big rock she leads me to General Mess. He's lying on his side. His eyes look sort of glassy. The scruffy fur on his side moves slowly up and down — so at least he's breathing. His front left paw is gone, and the leg is swollen — ugly — with flies buzzing around.

He looks half dead.

Arool stands over him, and her sides start heaving, and she vomits some food in front of the General's face for him to eat. The General sticks out his tongue, sort of dreamily, and flicks at the puddle, but that's all.

I want to help him and I don't know what to do. Except get him out of here. Off Burke's land. Back to the trailer. This is no place to die.

I step up to the General and reach out my hands.

Arool growls.

The General looks toward me, curls his lip and bares his teeth.

Looks like I ain't moving him. If he can bite off his own leg to get out of a trap, he can surely do some damage to my arm if I try to pick him up.

So I run.

I run down the gully. I run back along the fence line and through the barbed wire. I run along more fence past cows calmly chewing their cuds. I run down the hill to my trailer where I hop on my bike and ride into town to the phone in front of the store. I look in the Yellow Pages. Animal Doctors — see Veterinarians. Flipping pages. Veterinarians. A whole page of names. They're all in Pulgas Park or somewhere far away. I run into the store and find Kim. He knows everybody in town because they all come to his store sooner or later.

"Kim! I need a vet! Is there a vet in town?"

"No, Danny. No vet."

"What do people do when their dog gets hurt?"

"They take them to Pulgas Park. Do you have a hurt dog, Danny?"

"Yes."

"I could take you to Pulgas Park after I close the store. But then all the vets will be closed."

"I can't wait."

"You could try Dr. Vargas."

"He's a doctor?"

"He works with animals."

Kim didn't know his address, but he knew what street he lived on and what his house looked like. I found it.

I knocked on his door. Inside I heard music, violins.

The door opened. It was a man who was bald on top with white hair around the sides. He was wearing a red short-sleeve shirt and chewing on a piece of fried chicken — a drumstick — that he was holding in his hand.

"Are you Dr. Vargas?"

"Yes."

"I see it's your dinnertime and I'm sorry this ain't office hours, but this is an emergency."

Dr. Vargas stepped into his living room and turned down the violin music from his stereo. Then he came back to the door. "What's the emergency?" he said.

"He bit off his leg and now it's infected."

"A snakebite?"

"What snake?"

"Isn't there a snake?"

"No. It's a coy — " Wait a minute. If I tell him it's a coyote, he might not help me. These veterinarians do business with ranchers. "It's a dog."

"A snake bit the dog?"

"No. The dog bit his own leg off. He was caught in a trap."

"And there's no snake?"

"No."

"Oh." He took a last bite of chicken from the drumstick. "So what do you want from me?"

"Help."

"Why me?"

"Because Kim said you could help."

"Oh, yes. Kim. Fine man."

"So will you help?"

"If I can. Where is the dog?"

"He's — um — hiding."

"Can you call him?"

"He ain't here. He's in a gully. Under a rock."

"Can you bring him here?"

"He'll bite me if I try."

"Then can you take me there?"

"Well. Um."

"You don't want to take me there?"

"I guess I was wondering if you could just give me some medicine. For the dog."

"It would be better if I could see the leg. But then he probably wouldn't let me touch it anyway. And even if he did, I wouldn't know what to do."

"You wouldn't?"

"Why should I?"

"Ain't you a vet?"

"No."

"No?"

"No."

"Kim called you a *doctor*."

"Doctor of Philosophy."

"Philosophy? Oh no. What's *your* philosophy?"

"I'm a biologist. Specializing in Pulmonate Gastropods."

"What kind of a philosophy is that?"

"Slugs."

"You don't know dogs?"

"Slugs. Not dogs. Not cats. Not horses. Not cows. Pulmonate Gastropods. I've got samples of every species and subspecies on the West Coast. You want to see?"

"Not right now. I don't have time. I got a sick coyote. I mean dog. I was just hoping there was some medicine, but I guess you wouldn't have none. Not for dogs."

"Oh, I think I've got something you could use. For your, um, dog."

Dr. Vargas went into his house to a back room and came back with a brown plastic jar full of yellow pills.

"How big is this — this dog?"

I tried to show him with my hands.

"About regular size? Then give him six pills. All at once. It's a massive dose. It'll kill every bacteria in his leg — the good, the bad, and the ugly. Do it — oh, say — twice a day. I'm just guessing."

"Is this slug medicine?"

"It's a sulfa drug." He pointed at a large terrarium. "I was using it in an experiment on these *Ariolimax*."

"These what?"

"Banana slugs. As I said, there's one of each subspecies. Each kind."

I looked quickly at the terrarium.

"No, there ain't," I said.

"Ain't what? I mean — isn't what?"

"Each kind. There's no red spot."

"No species of *Ariolimax* has a red spot."

"I don't know about air-o-plane climax, but if you mean banana slug, I've seen them with red spots. Are you sure you're a biologist? You sure that's your philosophy?"

"Yes, I'm sure. Where did you see a banana slug with red spots?"

"Look. I'm in a hurry. I gotta go."

"Wait! I helped you. Now you help me. Where did you see a banana slug with red spots?"

"On the bottom of my shoe. When I stepped on it."

Dr. Vargas clapped his hands — angrily. "Where?" he said, almost shouting.

"Around town. I forget."

"This is important. Please. Try to remember."

"I don't know. Disappearing Creek. Somewhere near there. Look, Sir. I'm in a hurry. I got a sick . . . you know what. I'll tell you when I remember. But I gotta go."

"Disappearing Creek."

"Near. I'll tell you if I see any more and where. But I gotta go."

"Don't forget. Please."

"What do I owe you?"

"Nothing. Just — please — I want to see that slug."

And right then I remember. Law's house. His yard. But I don't want to take the time to explain where that is, so I don't say anything more about it.

I ride to the store and buy cream cheese and salami with my last dollar bills. Then I ride home and walk across the fields to General Mess in his gully under his rock. Miss Arool ain't there.

General Mess is sleeping. He opens his eyes when I come near. I stuff the six yellow pills into a wad of cream cheese and hold it out in front of his nose. He can't lift his head. He just looks at me and opens his mouth. Then he closes his eyes.

I push the cream cheese against his lips. With his tongue he rolls the wad into his mouth, chews once, twice — and swallows.

And I realize: He took my gift.

I climb to the top of his rock. The night comes on cloudy with no stars, windy but warm. I'm worried some animal will find the General and attack him when he can't defend himself. I'll be his guard. I'll stay here all night.

After a couple of hours, Miss Arool returns and lies down next to the General. I can hear her licking his leg.

The rock's too hard. I climb down and lay myself in the dirt, a few feet from the coyotes. Miss Arool growls at me a little bit, but then she goes back to licking the General's leg. Since they sleep together,

I wonder if they have the same dreams. Pop says if you sleep on the same pillow as your dog, you'll dream the dreams of your dog.

I hear a hoot owl across the meadow. I'm cold, lying in the dirt. I wiggle closer to the coyotes. Miss Arool stops her licking. I wiggle closer. I feel their heat. Closer. My head's right next to the General. And that's where we sleep.

21
COYOTE DREAMS

In my dream I run through grass over hills. I crawl in tunnels. I dig with my paws and poke my nose right into the earth to smell things I never could smell before: the scent of grasshoppers, the sweat of mice. I can hear like never before. I hear the footsteps of ants. The wind brings me the news. I can hear it from far away — the grumble of a car, the padding of footsteps, the bark of a dog. I dodge bullets. I run from dogs. I smell poison. I step in a trap, and I feel pain, pain, pain. I can't escape. I'm going to die.

I wake in the morning under a cloudy sky. The General is curled against my back. Arool is gone.

The leg looks no better. But no worse.

I take some salami from my pocket. I wrap it around six more yellow pills. When I wave it over the General's nose, he opens his eyes and tries to lift his head. It falls back. I push the salami against his lips, and he opens his mouth and feels it with his tongue. Then he curls his tongue around the salami, and — gulp — just like a frog — pulls it into his mouth. Slowly he chews while one eye studies me thoughtfully. Then he swallows. And closes his eye.

I figure I better go to school. For one thing, if I skip school, it calls attention to myself, and I'm supposed to bring a note from my father. Which would be difficult to arrange. For another, if I sit out here in this field and somebody comes along, they'll wonder what I'm doing here and come over to investigate, which is exactly what I don't want them to do.

Miss Arool comes trotting back to the rock. I toss her the rest of the salami. She looks at me suspiciously. Then she picks it up with her teeth and carries it over to General Mess.

"Take care of him, Miss Arool. I'll come back tonight."

All day I had coyotes on my mind. After school I could've looked for more work, but instead I ran to the gully. The air was drizzling in a heavy fog. A cold drizzle. I couldn't see to the hills or even to the end of the field.

The General lifted his head when I came near — and growled.

Not friendly. But a good sign. He must feel at least a little better.

I take a step closer, and Arool jumps up and snaps at me. So I stop. I stuff six yellow pills into a ball of cream cheese and toss it underhand to General Mess. It lands in the dirt by his head. He raises himself, though his belly never leaves the ground, and shuffles over a few inches, and grabs the cream cheese with his teeth. Of course it sticks to his teeth like a wad of gum, so he has to lick it off with his tongue.

Both the General and Arool are glaring at me. They don't seem too friendly when all I'm trying to do is save his life. I walk a little ways away and sit down. I'm wet. Drops of water are running out of my hair and over my face. My shirt is sticking to my shoulders. I'm shivering. I see Arool slip off across the field. There's sheep on the hill on the other side of the fence, but she ignores them. These coyotes ain't interested in sheep. Never were. Some get a taste for mutton, especially lamb — and some don't. And when they do, they don't just run them down for sport and leave bite marks all over the lamb's body the way Whiteknight did. They go straight for the head and kill it clean. And then they eat it.

I can't guard the General tonight. I'm already too cold and wet.

I walk back to the trailer. I read *Mad* magazines and try not to worry.

The milk is already gone. For dinner I eat the last piece of bread (the heel) and scrape the last glob of peanut butter from the jar. I spent all my money on the cream cheese and salami for General Mess.

I read another *Mad*.

Suddenly I hear footsteps on the front steps. Knock knock knock. Who could it be? Pop? No — Pop wouldn't knock.

I want to hide. If somebody is looking for Pop, I'll have to make up more lies. Easier if I just avoid them.

More knocking.

I get down on my hands and knees so whoever is out there can't see me, and I crawl to Pop's room where it's dark, and I peek out the window.

There on the front steps is Law.

I stick my head out the window. "Law! What are you doing here?"

He's wearing a blue backpack. He says, "I need a place to stay tonight. I'm running away."

"*You* want to stay with *me*?"

"Please."

"How'd you *find* me?"

"I asked that man at the grocery store."

"Kim?"

"Yes. Kim. May I sleep here tonight?"

"You could sleep on my father's bed. He — um — he has to work tonight, so he won't be needing it.

But there's no pillow. The rats tore it up."

"Rats?"

"They're gone, now."

I let him into the trailer. With the drizzle, the roof was leaking, dripping plop plop plop. Law wrinkled his nose. There's a musty smell the trailer gets whenever it's wet.

"Wow!" Law said. "This is *neat*."

"It is?"

Living in a trailer, you learn to make use of every inch. Besides the built-ins, Pop had added some more shelves and cabinets so that every bit of wall was covered. Law went around opening cabinet doors, saying, "This is *great*." Law thought our little eating nook looked cozy and fun, and he was knocked out by the way my bed folded up into the wall.

I'd thought the neat thing about Law's house was that you could see the entire wall of a room with *nothing* on it. It made you feel spacey.

"What happened to the television?" Law asked.

"Pop shot it."

"Really? Why?"

"Dsh," I said. I didn't know whether Law could understand.

"Wow," Law said, nodding his head. "My stepfather wouldn't even know how to *use* a gun."

I think Law understood. I had a feeling that Law's stepfather in his own way could do something —

whatever a rich person would do — that's like shooting a television. And whatever he did, I had a feeling he'd get away with it.

"You had dinner, Law?"

"No."

"I'm afraid I don't have anything."

"That's okay. I'll just eat some crackers or something."

"I don't have any crackers."

"Well. Milk. You know. Something."

"I don't have anything."

"Anything?"

"You bring any food in that backpack?"

"Just my soccer clothes."

"Where you running away to?"

"I don't know. I just had to get out. My stepfather. He yells at me. He yells at my mother. He drinks too much. He plays golf. He gripes about auditors and lawyers and accountants. He can't even find a job."

"You mean he doesn't work?"

"Not since he lost the savings and loan."

"He ran a bank?"

"I think he's going to move out. Or else Mother will move — and I'll go with her."

"I hope you stay, Law."

"Maybe we can stay in town. Maybe we could move in with *you*, Danny."

"Dsh. I don't think your mother would like it here."

"Why not? This is *neat*."

"It's dirty, Law. It's crowded. And we got no food. Hey. You have any money? We could go down to the store."

"I can't go. I'm sure they're looking for me. But you could go. I'll give you the money."

Law fished a wad of bills out of his pocket. He gave me a ten.

At the store I asked Kim if anybody had been looking for Law. He said no.

When I got back to the trailer, Law was exploring the built-in cabinets. He was standing in front of the cabinet where we keep our games — and he was holding a pile of Pop's poker chips.

"What are these?" he said.

I taught Law how to play poker. We ate taco chips with dip and drank root beer until late into the night, and we even ate the jelly doughnuts I'd bought for breakfast, and when I needed to I got out of my chair and walked a circle around it, and when we quit at midnight, I'd won one hundred and sixty-eight dollars in chips. But I didn't make him pay.

I didn't want to hose him.

That ain't my philosophy.

In the morning, I was up with the light. Law heard me.

"You can sleep some more," I told him. "I got to check on some animals."

"I'll go with you," he said. "What animals?"

"Dogs."

"You have dogs, Danny?"

"Sort of."

I was sick of lying. I was lying out of habit, even when I didn't need to. Why not tell him the truth? He wasn't going to blab about the coyotes to some rancher. And if I wanted Law to be my friend, I had to tell the truth.

"My mother won't let me have a dog," Law said. "She says they aren't clean."

"She's right. They ain't."

"*Life* isn't clean," Law said.

"Law? Those dogs of mine — they're coyotes. One's hurt. I need to see how he's doing."

There. I felt better. I felt cleaner, somehow. Law, meanwhile, didn't react at all. He didn't mind whether they were dogs or coyotes or jackals or hyenas. Everything about my life — how I lived and what I did — was new and interesting and exciting to Law.

I walked up the fence line. The sun was out. Little white puffy clouds of fog were sticking to the sides of some of the hills. Law followed, saying, "Wow, this is *great*. It's *beautiful* out here. You're so lucky, Danny, to live here."

"Who, me?"

"I wish I could live like you."

"*You* wish you could live like *me*?" Law's big roomy house — his whole rich world — was starting to seem more like a prison to me as I saw how little he knew about my world — the real world. Or is my world any more real than his? Maybe they're both real, only different.

We walked on. After a while Law said, "Uh — Danny? How much farther?"

"Another field."

"How much is a field?"

"Not much."

Breathing hard, he kept on walking.

We came to the gully — and the coyotes were gone.

The rain in the night had washed away any trace that they'd ever been there.

I didn't know how far General Mess could travel on three legs, still feeling sick. Maybe he and Miss Arool were still in the gully, just moved to a different hiding place.

Maybe he crawled off someplace to die.

Or maybe they went back to Hoggle's land, where they didn't have to worry about traps and where the cows would stir up the field mice, making the hunting easy. Maybe, even, they headed for the trailer, but I doubted it. Not after the way they growled at me.

They always shied away from the human race. With good reason. The General seemed to be willing to make an exception for me. Now — if he was alive — I didn't think he'd make that exception ever again. People are too dangerous. Too cruel. And they have too many weapons. Even though I was trying to save his life — and I think he knew it, or he wouldn't have eaten those pills — he still put me in the same scene with that trap, with the whole ordeal. He chewed off his own *leg*. That's how bad he wanted to live. And that's how bad he had to hurt, in order to live.

Now he'd have to learn to hunt all over again. He'd have to learn how to defend himself. On three legs. And he was tough enough to do it. Without my help.

But I wished I could still be his friend. I'd give him food until he was able to hunt. I could make it easier for him.

Maybe someday when they're in big trouble, I'll feel another nose against the back of my knee.

I reared back my head and howled.

Law looked startled.

Nobody answered.

"Is this what you came all this way to see?" Law said.

"They're gone," I said.

I led Law back across the fields and then up the road, through the fence and up the hill to the grave-yard with its view of the fields and farms and moun-tains. Law threw himself down on the ground and caught his breath. But then he sat up and said, "When I die, I hope I have a view like this."

The only view I was looking for was a three-legged coyote. But of course he wasn't there. The sun was high enough now to start raising steam from all the wet grass. It looked like the land was smoking. I led Law back down the hill. It was Saturday morning. Soccer Saturday.

I collected Hoggle's eggs.

"Wow," Law said. "Those are real eggs."

"Of course they're real." They were brown with little bits of feather and straw sticking to them.

"I mean," Law said, "when you buy them in the store, it's like they came out of a machine."

What I hadn't told Law yet was that since the propane tank was empty, we had no way to cook the eggs for breakfast. And no time to go to the store. In ten minutes, Mr. Barnaby would be coming to take me — us, now — to soccer. I wondered if Law would like how real eggs tasted if he had to suck them raw.

I walked into the trailer, trying to work up an appetite for sucking raw eggs, stepped into the kitchen — and it was different. I don't know how, but something was different. Somebody'd been in this kitchen since we left to check on the coyotes about two hours ago. Maybe just rats. Maybe . . . maybe Pop's home!

I dash to his room and throw open the door.

Nothing's changed. Same shredded pillow. Same beer cans on top of drawers. Same picture of my mother in her wedding dress. On a hook, the denim jacket:

WHEN I DIE I KNOW I'M GOING TO HEAVEN
BECAUSE I'VE ALREADY BEEN TO HELL.
KHE SANH.

Damn him! He tricked me again.

I slam the door shut to his room and stomp back to the kitchen and absentmindedly open the refrigerator door, even though I know there's nothing but ice cubes, just opening it out of habit, and I look inside . . . and I drop my hand off that refrigerator door like it was on fire.

There's food in there!

There's a carton of orange juice and another of milk. A package of hamburger meat and one of hot dogs. Cheddar cheese. Lettuce. Tomatoes.

The door, without my hand on it, shuts itself.

I look around the kitchen. The counter is clean. So's the table. That's what looked different. No crumbs. No ratdsh. And in the sink, like somebody left them there to dry, are six yellow apples. I open a cabinet. There's a loaf of bread, a package of hamburger buns, hot dog buns, and a box of Wheaties. In the other cabinet there's a bag of potato chips, a box of Ritz crackers, and Oreo cookies.

I look at Law. "Did you do this?"

"Do what?"

"This food. Where'd all this food come from?"

"I don't know."

We had to get dressed for soccer. We gulped down glasses of milk while changing our clothes.

I stuffed some clean clothes into an old backpack for after the game. I grabbed an apple and a handful of Ritz crackers, and we ran for the road.

And I was wondering, Who do I thank for this food? Luck? A shooting star? Is it really a gift? Or could it be — and suddenly a chill ran through me — could it be poison?

22
THE LOSERS

The whole Barnaby family was going to the game: Mr. and Mrs., plus Boone, Clover, and their little brother, Dale. In the back of the Volkswagen bus was a big net full of soccer balls and a stack of orange cones.

On the way to the game, Clover told me a boy can turn himself into a girl by kissing his elbow. And vice versa.

First came the Noodledood game. Mr. Barnaby let us do the coaching. Boone had figured out some tricks. Like, when he put Brian in as a forward, he put Clover in as goalie so they wouldn't be close enough to start tickling or talking or playing with each other and forget there was a game going on. And Babcock told Brian, "Don't touch any player on the other team."

"What if they bump into me?"

"Don't touch them," Babcock said.

"What if they're going for my ball?"

"Don't touch them."

"Why? Do I get a point?"

"No."

"Then what happens if I touch them?"

"We'll take you out of the game," Babcock said. "And you'll have to stand on the sidelines and hold hands with your sister."

Brian looked horrified. So did Geraldine.

"Okay," Brian said. "I won't."

With the rest of the Noodledoods, we were trying to teach shoulder tackles. With Brian, Babcock was afraid of a homicide.

After Brian scored three goals in the first half — and could have scored more, except he was so careful not to touch another player — Boone moved him to goalie and put Clover on the front line. The Noodledoods didn't score any goals in the second half, but neither did the other team, so the Noodledoods won, three to nothing.

Mr. Barnaby, instructed by Boone, invited all the Noodledood parents to stick around for the next game and cheer for the San Puerco Sucking Slime.

"I beg your pardon?" said the father of one of the Noodledood girls.

"The team," Mr. Barnaby said. "Their name is Slime."

"Why are they . . ."

"Never mind," Mr. Barnaby said.

They did stay.

In a town as small as San Puerco, most of the parents know most of the kids, even if the ages are different from their own kids', so they were interested in the game. We ended up with about two dozen parents, plus a dozen Noodledoods, plus a few other brothers and sisters cheering on the sidelines. And we needed it.

The other team was The Dragons. Walt had warned us, but still it was a shock to see how big they were. In fact, I wasn't sure which was the coach and which were the players until they ran out onto the field. Then I saw. The coach was the short one.

Walt grabbed my sleeve and pointed to the tallest Dragon, a kid who stood about six foot four and must've weighed two hundred pounds. "That's the coach's son," he said. "He's the one we have to stop."

"Why are you telling me?"

"Because I want you to stop him, Danny."

"How?"

"Like we said, Danny. Think positive."

I was thinking. But I didn't see one positive way to stop him. I didn't even see a negative way. He was too big.

We lined up for kickoff. I was opposite the big guy.

"How old are you?" I asked.

"Twelve," he said with a voice that wasn't nearly as big as his body.

"What's your name?"

"Stu," he said.

Steroid Stu, I'm thinking.

"What's *your* name?" Stu asked.

"Danny."

"Danny." He smiled. "I saw your mother eating out of a garbage can."

"You never seen my mother."

"Oh. I guess it must've been your grandmother."

Boone kicked off. In a split second a Dragon player had the ball. He passed. They worked the ball downfield. Dylan was playing fullback. Stu had the ball. Dylan challenged him. Stu nudged the ball around Dylan and pow! punched the ball into the corner of the goal out of the reach of Babcock.

"Yeah," somebody yelled. On the Dragon side, I saw two parents, one extra player, and the coach. That was all.

Babcock glared at Stu. He doesn't take kindly to people who score against him.

In the lot next to the soccer field, I saw a white Jaguar parking. Mrs. Livermore got out and walked to the field. She wore dark glasses and folded her arms across her chest. She was wearing white. She looked like a movie star.

"Hey Law," I said. "Look who's here."

"I know," he said.

"What are you gonna do?"

"Go home with her."

I'd thought he might turn tail and run, but I guess

he didn't want to. Maybe he'd had enough of running away. Or maybe he figured he'd made his point. Or, by coming to the game, maybe she'd made hers.

Boone kicked off again. The Dragons stole the ball, worked it downfield, passed to Stu. Stu kicked. Babcock made a dive — got it!

"HURRAY! NICE SAVE!" I heard from the sidelines.

"Lucky save, Fatso," Stu said. "Next time I'll kick your face."

Babcock punted. The Dragons got the ball. It looked like all the action was going to be on our end of the field. Stu shot a bullet — and scored.

"What took you so long?" I heard from the Dragon side.

Stu was smirking at Babcock.

Babcock just stood with his hands on his hips.

Boone kicked off with a short pass to Geraldine. I race down the sideline, and Geraldine lofts a pass. I hear cheering from our sideline: "YEAH! GREAT PASS!" The ball hits my chest, and I bring it down and get control. Meanwhile, Geraldine's running up the middle. I send her a pass. She's got a shot if she can get around one player: Stu. She dribbles to her left, gets clear — she's got a shot! — and Stu trips her. On purpose. To keep her from shooting. She falls flat on her side.

Like Walt warned us. They played dirty.

On the sideline I saw Brian hopping up and down,

mad. "He tripped my sister," Brian shouted. "He can't do that."

The ref blew the whistle. It was a penalty. Geraldine was given a direct kick. And she made it.

"HURRAY! GREAT SHOT! YAY GERALDINE! YAY SLIME!" shouted the people on our sideline.

The coach yelled at Stu, "Hey! You idiot! See what you cost us?"

I saw the Dragon coach didn't believe in positive coaching.

The Dragons kicked off. Stu passed the ball and then went running down the sidelines with me behind him. Everybody else was watching the ball on the other side of the field, but I was following Stu running right along the sideline in front of Brian — and Brian at the last second stuck out his foot — and Stu tripped and fell head over heels. He got back up and looked back, and Brian was standing with his arms on his hips, sticking out his tongue. Stu's arm was bleeding, scraped raw from the elbow to the wrist where it hit the ground. Stu glared at Brian, then ran back to join the action. He took a pass, tried a shot — and Dylan stole the ball.

"YEAH!" I heard from our sideline. "GREAT MOVE, DYLAN!"

Dylan passed to Boone. Boone got clobbered by a Dragon and fell to the ground. No whistle. The Dragons passed, and passed again, and — boom. Another goal.

"About time," somebody yelled on the Dragon side.

"That's making them work for it," Mr. Barnaby yelled from our side.

"Now get it back," Walt yelled.

"GO SLIME!" a bunch of people yelled together.

Strange to say, but I was having fun. The Dragons were bigger, stronger, faster, not to mention playing dirty, and they were beating us three to one. And yet every little thing we did right, every time we stole a pass or blocked a goal or made a good move, it felt like winning. And the sidelines cheered.

At halftime we were down, four to one. Walt huddled us together in front of the sidelines where everybody could hear, and we chewed on orange slices as Geraldine said, "They keep calling me names."

Walt said, "Like what?"

"I don't want to say."

"Does it bother you?"

"Yes."

"What do you want to do about it?"

"*Stomp* them."

"You did. You scored a point," Walt said. "You're doing a great job. Remember what we want to accomplish here. This team has never won by a margin of less than ten to one. If we can hold them under ten, that's a victory. I also thought it would be a victory if we could score just one goal. Well, we already did. Think how good it would feel to score another. Nobody's ever scored two goals against this team. You want to try?"

"Yes," Geraldine said, clenching her teeth.

"YES!" the parents all cheered.

Mrs. Livermore tapped Law on the shoulder. She took him aside and said a few words. He answered her, then ran back onto the field. So far, he still looked clean.

Mrs. Livermore was talking to Mr. Barnaby. She was pointing at me and shaking her head. Uh-oh, I thought. I'm in trouble now. I figured Law must have told her where he'd spent the night, and she was mad at me for letting him stay. But I couldn't worry about it. I had a soccer game to play.

The Dragons kicked off to begin the second half. We never touched the ball. In less than a minute, they scored another goal.

"THAT'S ALL RIGHT. YOU CAN DO IT," I heard from our sideline.

Dylan looked tired. So did Boone. The Dragons seemed rested. Maybe they got a fresh dose of steroids during halftime. Or maybe they could last longer, being bigger. I wasn't tired. I do so much running, or at least I did until I built my jalopybike, I could run for miles.

Boone kicked off. We took the ball a little way, then lost it. The Dragons worked toward our goal. We closed up. They passed it around, but they couldn't punch it in. We were holding them. Then somebody drilled a shot off Dylan's leg. The ball trickled toward a corner of the goal. Babcock raced for it. So did Stu. Stu kicked just as Babcock dove. They collided like a truck ramming a freight train. Babcock rolled over with the ball in his arms. Stu flew up in the air and came down knee first, then his chin crashed into the dirt.

For a second, he just lay there. Then, slowly, he pushed himself to his feet.

"You okay?" Babcock asked.

Stu didn't answer. He started jogging down the field — limping. Weaving slightly from side to side. The blood had dried on his arm.

The parents on our sideline started clapping, giving Stu a hand. Which bothered me some. Why should we be good sports to them unless they are to us? But I guess it's all part of having a positive attitude. I don't think Stu heard, anyway. His coach was yelling, "Shake it off! Hurry up! Hustle!"

One of the other Dragon players noticed the Slime parents giving Stu a hand. A black kid wearing purple sweatbands on his wrists. He stood with his hands on his hips, staring like he'd never seen soccer parents cheering a player on the opposite team.

The half went grinding on. They pushed us. They tripped us. They called us names. When we were down to the last five minutes, we were losing eight to one. And that was when another injury occurred. This time it was Law. He came out on the short end of a tussle with a Dragon, slipped or was pushed, I couldn't say which and the ref didn't see it, and Law was lying face down on the ground. The Dragon player, the boy with the purple sweatbands, stopped and looked down at him.

The Dragon coach yelled, "Play on!"

Walt was yelling, "Time! Ref! Injury!"

"Play on!" yelled the Dragon coach. "You! Get moving! The ref didn't call time!"

"He's hurt," the sweatband kid said to his coach.

Law was still lying there.

"Play on or you're off the team!" yelled the coach.

The sweatband kid looked at the coach. He looked at the ref, who was watching the action on the other side of the field. Then he glared directly at the coach and ran over to the ref. I saw him speaking to the ref and pointing at Law.

"Time out!" the ref called.

Walt and Mrs. Livermore ran onto the field. The sweatband kid, the Dragon, helped Walt carry Law off to the side. Then the sweatband kid sat down on our side of the field. And glared at his coach.

Mrs. Livermore held a bag of ice against Law's head. She was on her knees beside him in the dirt.

The game resumed. We were missing Law, and we had no subs. The Dragons sent in a sub for the sweatband kid who was sitting out on strike, so we were down one player. Stu moved to fullback.

In less than a minute, they kicked another goal. Nine to one.

Law was standing on the sideline. He looked all right. But he didn't come back into the game. Mrs.

Livermore was standing beside him. She had dirt on the knees of her white slacks. She held an arm around Law's shoulder. They were both watching the game. I thought to myself that maybe Law's running away for a night had been good for them both. I wondered if maybe someday Law and Mrs. Livermore would run away together — that is, away from Mr. Livermore. I had a feeling they would.

We kicked off. We lost the ball. The Dragons worked it down toward our goal. Suddenly Dylan got a clear, clean kick and the ball comes flying over everybody's heads to midfield where I'm waiting all alone. I kick toward the goal and go running after the ball. Stu comes running after me from the side. He's still limping. Geraldine runs down the field on the other side. It's me and Geraldine on a fast break against Stu and the goalie. Stu closes in. I pass to Geraldine. The goalie rushes out. Geraldine passes back to me — a chip shot, high in the air. Stu and I both jump for the ball. I try to head it, but Stu bumps me out of the way. Illegal, of course. But no whistle. The ball misses both of us and comes down at my side. It bounces up into the air again. I'm thinking: *My one chance for a goal this game, and I missed it.* After bumping me, Stu falls to the ground. I'm off balance. I twist my body, waving my arms, trying desperately to recover, but I have no control. My cleats come down on Stu's chest. The ball comes down from its bounce and hits me right on the butt. And shoots into the net.

Goal!

Everybody's shouting, "HURRAY! YEAH! GREAT SHOT! THAT'S USING YOUR BRAIN!"

The Dragon coach comes running down the sideline yelling, "Stu! You wimp! You let him score! You're doing laps for this."

Five seconds after the next kickoff, the ref blows his whistle. The game is over. The final score is nine to two.

Everybody on the Slime sideline is cheering and clapping. We do high fives, low fives; we shake cans of 7-Up and spray each other with the foam. And as we're celebrating, Stu hobbles up to us, running his first lap. His knee is swollen. Blood is caked on his arm. There's another cut on his chin. His jersey is torn where my cleats came down on his chest. He stops for a moment, panting for breath. He stares at us.

Clover's turning cartwheels. Babcock's whistling. Brian's throwing grass in the air. Geraldine's dancing a victory dance. Dylan's trying to join her, but he doesn't have the moves. Boone's hugging his mom and dad. Mrs. Livermore is smiling, though I don't think she really understands. I'm shaking hands with Walt, and everybody's saying congratulations.

"Hey," Stu says, but nobody pays any attention. "Hey. Don't you guys know you *lost*?"

He shakes his head, then jogs off, limping, on his laps.

23
IF WISHES
WERE PENNIES

Geraldine's mother dropped us off at the mall.

"So what do you want to do?" Geraldine asked.

"I dunno," I said. "What do you want to do?"

She shrugged. She stuck a hand in her big ball of hair. She seemed nervous.

I'd never seen her nervous before. I said, "I guess I'm sort of hungry. You want to eat?"

"Okay."

"I got no money, Geraldine."

"I told you I'd pay. My mother gave me some money."

We went to Carl's Jr. Geraldine ordered a burger and a Coke. I ordered a double burger, strawberry shake, stuffed potato with cheese, and two cookies.

"Can you really eat all that?" Geraldine asked.

"I'm hungry."

We sat at a table. I guess neither of us knew what to say. Geraldine looked at her fingernails. I slid around in my seat, trying to get comfortable.

Somebody had to say something, so I said, "Great soccer game, huh?"

"You know what we did?" Geraldine said, looking up from her fingernails. "We made them think they lost."

"That ain't all," I said. "We felt like we won. I guess sometimes losing can feel like winning."

"It was you and me who scored. We're a combo."

"The whole team played hard. Dylan made some plays."

"So?"

"Dylan's a good kid. He likes you, you know."

"I noticed." She sneered.

"He wanted to ask you out. He's supposed to be here instead of me."

"So why did *you* call instead of *him*?"

"He was afraid you'd say no."

"He's right."

"Why are you so hard on him?"

"Because he had you call instead of asking for himself. He's always doing dumb things like that. I knew what you were calling about. I just pretended I didn't understand."

"So why am I here?"

"To make him mad."

"So look what happened. I didn't want to ask you. But I'm here. And you didn't want me, you just wanted to make Dylan mad. So neither of us wanted to be here. This whole thing — you and me being here — this is just an *accident*."

"Not really." She smiled, like she knew some secret. "But anyway, we're here. And my mother gave me some money, and if I don't spend it, I have to give it back."

"You want to go shopping? I could just stay here."

"No." She looked at me, then quickly looked away. "I mean, I'd rather we did something. I mean, together."

I looked down at my hamburger. I said, "So would I." Then I looked up at her and saw she was smiling. As soon as I looked at her, though, she wiped off the smile and looked down at her food.

Geraldine took a bite of her burger, then pushed it away. I ripped into my food. I felt juices trickling down my chin. I didn't care. I was hungry.

"That was neat having everybody cheering for us," Geraldine said. "Even my mother cheered. Even my *brother*."

"He did more than cheer," I said, and I told Geraldine about Brian tripping Steroid Stu as he was running along the sideline.

Geraldine laughed. "Brian did that? That wasn't *positive*."

"Nope. But it felt good."

"Danny? Why didn't your parents come to the game?"

"Pop's busy. He — he had to go to the hospital. To see somebody."

When I lie, I like to pick one that's close to the truth. But this one was a mistake because Geraldine said, "Couldn't he have waited until after the game?"

"No."

"Why not? What hospital?"

"VA."

Geraldine looked at me hard. "Who's he visiting?"

"I forget."

"Why couldn't he wait until after the game? Couldn't he visit the VA in the afternoon?"

"Maybe. I don't know."

Geraldine was still studying me. It made me nervous. She said, "You're the only kid on our team who didn't have a parent there. Seems kind of curious."

"You wouldn't want my father there."

"Why not?"

"He loses his head. If he saw the way some of those kids was playing, he'd go stomping right onto the field and start punching them out. He'd punch the ref, too. He hates refs."

"Why?"

"He hates anybody like that. Cops. Refs. Lifeguards. And he hates anybody in a coat and tie."

"Why?"

"Because he was hurt in the war. In Vietnam. He's got a head limp."

"Was he shot?"

"No. It's not that kind of limp."

"So what does being hurt in a war — having a limp like you say — what does that have to do with hating referees and lifeguards?"

"I guess they remind him of being in the army. People ordering him what to do."

"Does he *embarrass* you sometimes?"

"Lots of times."

"Don't you wish sometimes your parents would just *go away*?"

I was sucking on the milk shake when she said that, and I almost choked. "No," I said.

"I do."

"My mother went away already. She's dead."

"Oh. I'm sorry, Danny. I didn't mean I wished they were *dead*."

"Pop always left me alone. I always wished I had more of him, not less."

"At least you've got a father," Geraldine said, picking at her hair.

"You don't?"

"Not really. He lives in Ohio. They divorced. I'm not allowed to see him."

"That's too bad."

"No. I'm glad. I don't want to see him."

"You don't like him?"

"He went away. He couldn't've liked *us* much, to do that."

"Is this crazy? People who don't got parents wish they did. And people who got them wish they didn't."

"Not everybody," Geraldine said. "Some kids are lucky."

I finished my food. Geraldine only took the one bite out of her burger.

"So what do you want to do?" she asked.

"I want another burger." So I got one.

When I sat down again, Geraldine said, "I guess parents are all right. I mean, somebody's got to take you to flute lesson."

"I never had no flute lesson."

"That's just an example. I mean, it's handy to have a parent when you want to go skiing."

"You ski?"

"Sure."

"What's it like?"

"You've never been skiing, Danny?"

"No."

"It's fun. Maybe we could take you this winter. It's better than Disneyland."

"I never been to Disneyland."

"Danny! Don't you ever go anywhere?"

"We got no car."

"You can't live without a car."

"Then I must be dead."

"I've never seen a dead person eat so much food."

"I ain't dead. I'm a coyote."

"What does that mean?"

"You ever seen a coyote?"

"No."

"They're wild. Smart. They're clowns. They work in pairs. And they do whatever they got to do. They survive. Just call me Danny Coyote."

Geraldine leaned toward me across the table. She said, "Do you work in a pair, Danny?"

"No."

Softly she said, "When you play soccer you do. You and me."

"That's different."

She leaned back and looked away. Staring at a potted plant, she said, "Are you a clown, Danny?"

"Not usually. Not if I can help it."

"Why do coyotes act like clowns?"

"They got reasons. Like people. When people act crazy, maybe they got reasons, too." I was thinking of Pop.

"How do you know about coyotes, Danny?"

"From Pop. And I seen 'em."

Now she looked back at me. "Really? Where?"

"It's . . . kind of a secret."

She leaned forward again. "I won't tell."

I leaned forward to meet her in the middle of the table. Our heads were just inches apart. Her hair smelled like dust. I said, "They used to live right under my trailer."

She whispered, "Where'd they go?"

"I wish I knew."

She furrowed her eyebrows. She whispered, "I wonder what a coyote dreams."

"Why?"

"When I try to imagine how another person lives, I try to imagine what they must dream at night. Animals dream, too, you know. So I wonder what a coyote dreams about."

"I know what they dream." I sat back. "Being shot at. Eating poison. Chased by dogs. Getting caught in a trap and having to break his own leg off to get free. Staying awake, because he don't want to dream. That's a coyote."

"You think it's all *bad* dreams?"

"What else is there?"

Geraldine was looking right into my eyes. She said, "Is that you, Danny?"

"Dsh."

"That's *awful*."

"I'm okay. It's worse with Pop."

"What's he dream about?"

"War."

"What do you dream about?"

"Stuff."

"What stuff?"

"Never mind."

"War?"

"Sort of. I guess. Yeah. Maybe." Actually, I'd never thought of it that way before. I never made the connection.

Me and Pop, maybe we both had limps in the

head. Only his was worse. And I wasn't going to sit around feeling sorry for myself.

Geraldine started drawing something on the tabletop with her fingertip. She wasn't looking at me when she said, "I hope your father gets out of the hospital soon."

"Geraldine! I told you. He's just visiting."

She looked up from her drawing. She said, "I'm pretty good at faces."

"My face?"

"That, and some stuff you said today. I figured it out." Geraldine went back to running her finger over the tabletop. "So who's taking care of you?"

"Nobody."

"How do you feed yourself?"

"I told you. I'm a coyote."

"You could ask for help, Danny Coyote."

"If I ask for help, I end up in an orphan home."

"Maybe not. Maybe somebody would just help."

"Coyotes don't take no help. They're *wild*."

"What if their life depended on it?"

"Then . . . they might take it."

Geraldine laid her hands flat on the tabletop. No rings on her fingers. She didn't wear jewelry or makeup. She gave me a serious look and said, "Danny, you're no coyote. You're not wild. You're a human being."

"I can be wild, too."

"People help people."

"*Some* people help *some* people. You gotta know

which is which. You gotta be *street*."

"I know."

"You don't know. How could you know?"

"We all have limps, Danny. We've all been hurt."

I thought of Geraldine's father. That must've hurt, when he moved out. Or maybe it hurt more, living with him. Like Law and his stepfather.

Geraldine was smiling. She said, "You ever been out with a girl before?"

"No."

"I've never been on a date, either."

"Is this a date, Geraldine?"

She shrugged. She said, "If it is, do you know that all you've done on this date is *eat*?"

"So what do you want to do?"

"I don't know, Danny. What do you want to do?"

"Dsh."

"What?"

"Let's get some ice cream."

We got cones. I walked around the mall with Geraldine. We looked in windows. We chased a pigeon who kept just out of our reach. We came to a fountain where some metal flamingos were spitting water into a pool. We sat down at the edge of the pool, and I saw something glinting under the water. Coins.

"Geraldine? Could I borrow a penny?"

She gave me one.

I dropped it into the water of the fountain, then waited for the surface to calm down so I could see my reflection — because, of course, you can't make a wish until you see your reflection clearly. But when the ripples stopped, what I saw wasn't my own face but Geraldine's, looking over my shoulder. And that got me so confused that I forgot to make a wish. Or maybe Geraldine was my wish.

On the back of my hand I saw one short black hair. An eyelash. Somebody's eyelash had fallen onto the back of my hand. Was it mine? Or Geraldine's? I closed my eyes. I made a wish. I took a deep breath, and I blew. When I opened my eyes, the eyelash was gone.

This time, I knew what I had wished. I wished I was rich. I wished Geraldine would stay my friend. I wished Pop would come home.

"Hey." A man's voice. I looked behind me and saw blue pants, a blue shirt, a badge, a walkie-talkie. A security guard. "Hey," he said. "Can't you read the sign?"

He was pointing at a plaque that said,

PLEASE DO NOT PUT COINS IN FOUNTAIN.

"I was making a wish," I said.

"It costs them thousands of dollars a year to clean all the coins out of these fountains. It's a *nuisance*."

I wondered if I was under arrest. I looked around. Maybe I could run away. I could outrun this guy. Maybe I could circle around and switch off with

Geraldine, hide in a bush and wait until he's tired, and then run him into a fence.

I felt Geraldine's hand on my shoulder. "Danny," she said, "get the penny."

There's no bushes in a mall. No fence.

And no wishes.

"I'm sorry," I said. "I'll take it out."

"You do that."

I reached into the water. It was cold. My hand touched bottom and scooped up a pile. I brought it out of the water and saw what I'd captured: one nickel, one dime, nine pennies, a plastic bread-wrapper closer, a brass screw, and a wad of gum. I dropped the garbage in a trash can and the coins in my pocket. One penny I gave back to Geraldine.

I guess it canceled my wish.

"Can I get more?" I said to the guard.

"Sure," he said. "Clean it all out if you want to."

I scooped again. And again. There was good money in there. I threw away the garbage and kept the coins. Mostly pennies. I worked my way around the edge of the pool. The wet coins in my pocket made a dark circle on my pants.

Geraldine helped scoop up some coins, but she gave them all to me. Pounds of pennies. Both my front pockets were stuffed.

"Think I got enough pennies for a movie ticket?"

"Keep it. I've got to spend my mom's money, or she'll take it back."

We watched something about good guys and bad

guys crashing cars and shooting at each other and jumping through glass windows in slow motion. There was one long kissing scene, which gave me time to go to the lobby and get popcorn and not miss anything.

When we came out, we wandered back to the fountain. Geraldine looked at the metal flamingos and said, "Danny? Were you thinking about running away from that security guard?"

"Uh-huh."

"I'm glad you didn't."

"You stopped me. When you put your hand on my shoulder."

"Like this?" she said, and she put her hand on my shoulder again.

I put a hand on her shoulder, too. I said, "Thanks for being my partner."

She said, "Thanks for being mine."

It was time to meet her mother for the ride home. I was thinking: This is the weirdest date I ever had.

Of course, it's the only one, too.

Back home, there's no coyotes. I check the refrigerator to make sure the food's still there. Yep. Cabinets, too. Whoever put it there didn't take it back. It's put there for me.

It ain't poison.

It ain't bait.

And this ain't no trap.

Somebody wants to help me. And I ought to stop

acting like a stubborn coyote. Maybe what's poison is thinking I'm street. Poison is thinking I got to do everything for myself, thinking everybody wants to send me to some orphan home with the likes of Big Al.

Maybe it's time my war was over. The right time, as Pop would say. Maybe I can make that choice — to stop my war. Maybe, with a little help from my friends.

I want to go look for General Mess and Miss Arool. It's a cool night. I walk into my father's room, and — something I never did before — I take his jacket off the hook on the wall. It's big. But I like the feel. I like the words, too, the way they feel on my back.

Be my friend, big jacket. Keep me warm tonight.

Without a flashlight I run up the fence line and across the fields to the gully. I give a good howl, but I get no answer, just a lizard scuttling under a rock. I go to the road, through the barbed wire and up the hill to the graveyard. I give another howl. No answer. And no ghosts, either. I pick a dandelion and blow all the seeds off the stem. They catch the wind and fly to the stars.

Go, little seeds. Good things are coming.

24
A GOOD DAY
FOR RAINBOWS

I'm awake as soon as there's light, as usual, but instead of hopping right out of bed I do something different. I lie there. I'm thinking about Geraldine. And I'm remembering something about how I slept: I didn't have any dreams that I can recollect. No scary stuff. I must have dreamed, but nothing woke me up sweating with my heart pounding and big pictures in my head. I just went to sleep, and I slept, and I probably had some average workaday dreams, and when I had enough sleep, I woke up. First time that's happened since Pop went away.

When I finally do get up, I collect the eggs and then make a circle of rocks in front of the trailer and build a fire. When it burns down to coals, I fry me a hamburger and scramble some eggs. It's cloudy and cool, so I wear Pop's jacket.

As I ate, the sky cleared and the sun came out. Then as I finished, the sky covered over again. The clouds were rolling along.

I thought I'd ride my jalopybike over to Geraldine's house and see if anything was happening. Before I got there, though, I met Dr. Vargas. He was walking, so I caught up with him on the bike.

"Well, hello," he said. "How's your — uh — dog?" And he grinned.

"Gone," I said.

He frowned. "Gone as in dead and gone?"

"Just gone. He took pills that night you gave them to me, then more in the morning, then that night again, but then the next morning he was gone. I didn't think he could even *walk*."

"Perhaps you'll see his tracks. They'll be quite distinctive, having only three legs." Dr. Vargas grinned. "Perhaps you'll see the tracks of little *crutches*."

The sun came out again.

Dr. Vargas turned serious-looking. He said, "I was just going back to Disappearing Creek. I still haven't found any of those red-spotted *Ariolimax* you said were near there. Have you see any more?"

"No." And then I remembered. "Follow me," I said. "I'll show you where I saw them."

"Oh that would be *wonderful*."

The sun went behind a cloud, a big one.

I walked alongside my bike. I was worried about what would happen at the Livermores' house. I didn't know whether they knew where Law had spent the night when he ran away and whether they'd be mad at me if they did know. But I figured I'd have to face up to it sooner or later, so I might as well face it now.

We came to the intersection with another street, and along came Babcock walking toward us carrying a big bag of popcorn.

"Going to feed the ducks?" I asked. Lots of times I'd seen Babcock throwing popcorn to the ducks down at the pond.

"That's what my parents think," Babcock said. He took a handful from the bag and stuffed it in his mouth. He said. "The ducks like it plain, but I like it with butter and cheese."

"You still on that diet?"

"Yes. But I haven't lost any weight." He smiled, with a look of satisfaction.

I said, "We're going to look at some slugs. You want to come?"

"Okay," he said.

"Babcock," I said, "you're the only person I can think of who would accept an invitation to go look at some slugs."

"What about me?" Dr. Vargas said. "Aren't I a person?"

"Oh. Of course. I forgot. Babcock, this is Dr. Vargas. He likes slugs."

"Very pleased to meet you," Dr. Vargas said.

As we walked by the pond, all the ducks spotted

Babcock with his bag of popcorn and came padding up the street after us, quacking.

"They seem to think you're going to feed them," Dr. Vargas said.

"Usually, I do," Babcock said.

The goose waddled up and joined the ducks. When he saw that Babcock wasn't sharing the popcorn, he started honking with a fury. It sounded as if he was cussing Babcock out in goose language. Meanwhile the ducks had run around in front of Babcock so he couldn't take a step without kicking them.

Babcock stopped. He ate another handful of popcorn.

Suddenly the goose lunged and took a peck — a nip, actually — at Babcock's leg.

"Ow!" Babcock said.

Honk! said the goose.

"Oh, all right," Babcock said, and he dumped the rest of the popcorn onto the ground.

Quack quack! said the ducks, and it sounded like "Thank you" — the way it would sound if you said it holding your nose.

We walked on.

"Babcock talks to dragonflies," I said.

"What do you say?" Dr. Vargas asked.

"Well," Babcock said. He shrugged. "You know."

"Dr. Vargas?" I said. "Do you talk to slugs?"

"If I do," Dr. Vargas said, "I try not to let anyone know about it."

Babcock was keeping an eye on the sky. He said to me, "It looks like a good day for rainbows."

"What do you mean?"

"I mean, if you keep your eye out today, you're likely to see rainbows."

"You can predict rainbows?"

"Sure. Anybody can."

Just then the sun came out again from behind a cloud.

We walked along Creek Road, up the Livermores' driveway, and I knocked on the front door. Babcock and Dr. Vargas stood a few steps behind me.

Mrs. Livermore opened the door. "Well if it isn't Danny," she said. "What a pleasant surprise."

"Mrs. Livermore, I'm sorry," I said. "That is, if you're mad at me."

"Why should I be mad at you? I want to thank you. Thank you for letting Law spend the night at your — um — house."

"He told you?"

"Oh I already knew. That man at the grocery store. Kim. He told me."

"So you knew where he was and you didn't come get him?"

"I knew he'd be safe with you, Danny. You know how to take care of yourself. I can *see* that."

I told her we wanted to look for slugs in her yard.

"You *want* to find slugs?" she said. "Can you get rid of them?"

"He just wants to see them," I said. "He's a philosophy doctor."

She said he was welcome to look, and as far as she was concerned, he could take them all away with him.

Law came to the door. "What are you doing?" he said.

"Looking for slugs. You want to help?"

Law came outside and put on his shoes.

"Great yard you have here," Babcock said.

"I want to make it into a soccer field," Law said.

"You should dig a pond," Babcock said. "This would be a nice place for a pond."

"Why would I want a pond?" Law said.

"Because then you could have dragonflies," Babcock said. "And fish. And ducks. And *everything*."

"I'd rather have a soccer field," Law said.

"Eureka!" Dr. Vargas shouted. He held up a slug between his fingers. It was about six inches long, yellow with a red spot. He peered at it closely, turning it in his fingers while the slug tried to wiggle and twist and slime itself free.

"It's an entirely unknown species," Dr. Vargas said. "Not *dolichophallus* or *californicus* or *stramineus* or *brachyphallus*, and certainly not *columbianus*."

The slug had stopped wiggling and was now extending its tentacles toward Dr. Vargas's face, as if it were studying him. Maybe Dr. Vargas was a new species that the slug had never seen before, either.

"Since I discovered it," Dr. Vargas said, "I get to name it."

"I discovered it before you did," I said.

"That's true. What would you name this new species?"

"Law saw it before I did. I'd name it after Law. Law Livermore."

"*Ariolimax Livermorus.* How's that?" Dr. Vargas said.

"I'll just call it the red-spot," I said.

"You're naming a slug after *me*?" Law said.

"Is that all right? It's quite an honor."

"My name isn't Livermore," Law said.

"It isn't?" I said. "But your parents — "

"My mother remarried. She took my stepfather's last name. But I still have my father's name. I wouldn't take my stepfather's name if you held a gun to my head."

"So what's your name?" I said.

"Deerbourne."

"*Ariolimax Deerbournus.* A lovely name," Dr. Vargas said.

"Thank you," Law said.

"They may only live in this one small part of town," Dr. Vargas said. "They may only live in this one *yard*." Dr. Vargas looked at Law with admiration. "You're a lucky young man. You live in an ecosystem that must be unique to this world. I'll have to study this land. I need to determine their diet and breeding habits."

"Can I help?" Law asked. "Can I use it as a science project?"

"You'll win first prize," Dr. Vargas said. "Who else can say they helped discover a totally new species of animal? And gave it their name?"

"What should I do?"

"First, let's determine the extent of their habitat. Let's see where they live."

We spread out — Law, Dr. Vargas, Babcock, and me. We found red-spotted slugs everywhere that the soil was damp, which was almost everywhere in Law's yard and not at all beyond it. Law's yard was the whole flat bottomland between two hills. The house itself was slightly higher than the yard, built at the base of the hill where it seemed to be dry.

"There must be an underground water supply," Dr. Vargas said. "Something is keeping it green here. This is the valley of Disappearing Creek. Maybe it's under here somewhere."

We were interrupted by a rumbling and a clanking in the driveway.

Hoggle. With his tractor.

"Oh no," Law said.

"What is going on?" Dr. Vargas said.

Hoggle drove the tractor off his trailer. It beeped as he backed it up, and there was a spark arrestor on the smokestack.

Babcock ran up to Hoggle. "The taillight on your trailer doesn't work," he said.

"So write me a ticket," Hoggle said. And he drove the tractor into the yard.

Dr. Vargas shouted. "What do you think you're doing?"

"Digging a swimming pool," Hoggle said.

"Right here?"

"Right here. Then they're gonna pour a concrete patio all around it — all over the yard. They're gonna turn this old patch of weeds into something *nice*."

"But you can't! This is a *unique* habitat. There's an endangered species here. It's so rare, we never even *found* it until today. We must make this yard a *sanctuary*."

Hoggle looked at Law and said, "Is this another of your delaying tactics?"

Law shook his head. "I've never even seen this guy before. But he's right. There's an endangered species here. The red-spotted slug. *Deerbournus*."

"*Slug*?" Hoggle laughed. "Gimme a *break*. You've run me through enough hoops already. I've got the geology report, I've got the permit, I've got all the papers."

"No you don't." Babcock stepped forward. He pushed his glasses up on his nose as if he was cocking a weapon. He squared his shoulders and stood up straight and tall and said, "You'll have to file an Environmental Impact Report."

"Here's my impact report," Hoggle said, and he lowered the blade of the tractor. The engine roared. The tractor lurched forward and began cutting a six-foot-wide lane of raw dirt and tractor tracks, shoving the grass and wildflowers and weeds — and any slugs — out of the way. Two quail exploded out of the brush and flapped away. A rabbit suddenly leaped and was gone.

Dr. Vargas said, "I'll call somebody. I'll get a court order."

"It's Sunday," Law said in a flat voice. "You can't get anything today."

Hoggle had now reached the site where the swimming pool was to be, and he started scooping a hole.

Law ran to the house, whipped off his shoes at the front door, and ran inside.

It was starting to rain. A light mist was coming down. Hoggle kept right on digging. From where I was standing, it looked as if the ground was bouncing under the tractor — almost as if it was hollow under there. The tractor was shaking the earth. I could feel it where I was standing. Hoggle was rattling in his seat. I didn't see how a man with a bad back could stand it — except that he was going to make a killing on the job. Cracks were forming in the dirt, making a circle around where he was excavating.

Law came out of the house with his mother and stepfather.

Mr. Livermore stopped and stared at Hoggle's tractor. Only the spark arrestor and backup beeper were new. Otherwise, it was the same old rusty bucket of junk it had always been. I guess Mr. Livermore had never seen it before.

Mr. Livermore walked up to Dr. Vargas. For the first time I noticed how short Mr. Livermore was. He only came up to Dr. Vargas's chin.

"My son tells me you've made some sort of a discovery on my land," Mr. Livermore said.

"Yes," Dr. Vargas said. "An entirely new species of animal never before known to man."

"I'd rather you discovered oil," Mr. Livermore said.

"This is more precious than oil," Dr. Vargas said.

"Not in dollars and cents, it isn't," Mr. Livermore said.

"Oh I think it is," Dr. Vargas said. "No amount of money could replace it if it were to become extinct."

"What is it?"

"*Ariolimax*," Dr. Vargas said.

"What?"

Before Dr. Vargas could say more, Law broke in and said, "It's named *Ariolimax Livermorus*."

Dr. Vargas raised an eyebrow toward Law and said, "But I thought we named it — "

"*Livermorus*," Law said firmly.

"*Livermorus?*" Mr. Livermore said.

"It's named after you, Father," Law said.

"What a lovely name," Mr. Livermore said. He looked pleased. "And just what is this *Livermorus*?"

"A Pulmonate Gastropod."

"A what?"

Just then there was a rumbling sound. The first thing I thought was: earthquake!

We all looked around.

Hoggle cried out — a yelp like a dog when you step on his tail.

It wasn't an earthquake. It was the land collapsing under the tractor. I saw the top of the tractor, with Hoggle on it, tilting to the side at a crazy angle and sinking right out of sight.

Hoggle stood on the seat. He leaped to the side of the hole. It was caving in as he was trying to cling to it. He scrambled on his hands and knees over rocks and falling dirt. We ran to the side of the hole. Dr. Vargas knelt at the edge of the pit and reached out a hand. Hoggle leaned forward and grabbed the hand. His weight nearly pulled Dr. Vargas into the hole. I grabbed Dr. Vargas at the shoulders, and Babcock grabbed me by the waist. We pulled like a tug-of-war — and won — and our prize was a dirty, out of breath, frightened Henry Hoggle.

The tractor lay sideways in an underground cavern. It gave a last shuddering sigh as water from the cavern rose, and more dirt fell, and quickly just one corner of the tractor was visible at the bottom of a new, deep, suddenly permanent-looking pond: a sinkhole, maybe twenty feet across. The water rose to a level about a foot below the top of the hole, then stopped.

It all happened so fast, we could only stand there, staring. Hoggle was catching his breath.

Dr. Vargas wiped his hands on the side of his pants. "I believe Disappearing Creek," he said, "has just reappeared."

"My God," Hoggle said. "I thought I was done for."

"What a great pond!" Babcock said. "Just what you needed!"

I noticed that the rain had stopped. I looked up, and just as Babcock had predicted, there was a rainbow spreading out over the mountains.

Mrs. Livermore looked at Hoggle, who was covered with dirt, and said, "Are you all right?"

Hoggle ran his hands over his body. "Nothing broken," he said. "Except for one old piece-of-crap tractor." He sighed. "Got me some bruises, though. That's more excitement than an old body like this should have to stand. Take my advice, you people. Don't ever get old." From his pocket he pulled out a crushed pack of cigarettes.

Mr. Livermore looked at the cigarette — which was right at his eye level — with stern disapproval. He said, "I hope you don't expect me to pay for any of this."

Hoggle's eyebrows shot upward. "Hey. Now look," Hoggle said. "I came here in good faith and started the job just as we agreed, in spite of all the extra problems your son created. Of course I can't finish it, but I expect some — "

"Not one penny," Mr. Livermore said.

"I worked. I didn't finish, but I worked. I lost a tractor."

"That wasn't a tractor. That was a rolling wreck. If I'd seen the condition of your equipment before I hired you I never would have — "

"Hey. It worked."

"What about that geologist's report? It said I had a normal piece of land. What kind of tests did he run out here?"

"Geology reports are a waste of time," Hoggle said. "All they do — "

"That hole is a waste of time, Mr. Hoggle. A geologist should have told me there was an underground creek there. I hired you to give me a swimming pool. Not a sinkhole."

"So I ran into some problems. It happens with every job."

"I've been talking to some of your other jobs. You've cheated every person who ever hired you."

"I don't cheat. That's just business."

"Do you have a business license?"

"No. But I've been doing business for — "

"Do you have a contractor's license?"

"No. But I've been doing — "

"Not one penny, Mr. Hoggle."

Babcock walked around the edge of the new pond. Dr. Vargas followed, and I followed him. Hoggle and Mr. Livermore continued to argue. Law was talking to his mother. As I came near them, Mrs. Livermore was saying, "You're a smooth operator, Law, naming that little beast after your father."

"So you'll do it?" Law said.

Mrs. Livermore sighed. She said, "I've given money to save baby seals. Cute, fuzzy, baby seals. I've given money to save dolphins. They have such nice smiles. And they're so smart. I gave money to help save the rain forests, and now, of all things, of all *things* . . ."

"I'm sure Father will find some tax advantages to creating a wildlife refuge," Law said.

"I'm sure he will," Mrs. Livermore said. "Especially when the wildlife is named after him."

"Will you do me a favor, Mother? Will you be the one to break the news to him what a Pulmonate Gastropod is?"

"Ugh. I hate them. Even the *name* is ugly."

"It's for the good of the planet, Mother."

I realized that Mrs. Livermore was choosing to create a sanctuary. I was thinking how much the world — even down to the slugs — depends on the choices people make.

And then suddenly I realized something else. I walked over to Mrs. Livermore and said, "Thank you for the food you left in my trailer."

"You're welcome, Danny."

Babcock was standing with his hands on his hips. Some bubbles were rising from where the tractor was buried under the water. They wiggled in a line up to the surface, then spread over the water like foam on a giant soda pop.

"I was right," Babcock said. "This is definitely a good day for rainbows."

25

WHERE THE SLUG AND THE COYOTE PLAY

As I was riding my jalopybike through the farmyard on the way to the trailer, Hoggle saw me and waved me down. I could see right away he was in a terrible mood.

"Where's your father?" he said.

"I don't know."

"Is he too busy to pay the rent? It's three weeks late. You tell him I want that money now. Or you guys can clear out of here. And starting next month, I'm raising the rent by a hundred dollars a month. Since he never does any work around here, he's got to pay more. You tell him that. You hear?"

"I hear."

I turned the bike around, rode into town, and called Tommy.

No answer.

After I hung up the phone, I saw a red Trans Am parked in front of the store. One of the fenders looked like it got in a fight with a utility pole — and lost. The door opened, and out stepped Damon Goodey, wearing sunglasses, gold chains, silk shirt, and a diamond pinkie ring.

Goodey looked me up and down. I was wearing my father's denim jacket — the war jacket with the message on back. The sleeves hung down over my hands. There were holes in the knees of my pants. My little toe waggled out the sides of my old Nikes.

"You lookin' for me?" Goodey asked.

Rent. I could pay it, working for Goodey. Pay the rent and a whole lot more.

"No," I said. "I ain't looking for you."

"You had your chance," Goodey said and without another word, he walked by me and into the store.

I could've made a lot of money working for him. And I would've had to bite my own leg off to get out of his trap. If I got out at all.

I was thinking, there's a lot of traps in this life. There's poison bait and shotguns to dodge. I guess growing up is learning to make the right choices. And I'm ready to make some now, myself.

I think I'll go over to Geraldine's house. See what's cooking.

At night I climbed the hill to the little graveyard. The wind was sweeping waves through the grass. Clouds shot across the sky. The night was wild, fresh, tingly — and dark. There was no moon, just sharp bright stars in the spaces between the clouds. I was looking for coyotes, but I knew on a night like this I wouldn't see them unless they wanted me to. And I wasn't sure they wanted, ever again. Even though Miss Arool had come to me for help with a nose against the back of my knee, even though I'd tried to help the General with pills and salami and cream cheese, even though they knew I wanted to be their friend and the General, at least, had wanted to be mine, they couldn't get around the fact that I was a human being. And human beings set traps. Human beings use poison. Human beings shoot guns. I couldn't blame them for staying away. But I wanted to see them. I wanted to know if the General was still alive. And if he died, would Miss Arool stay around? Would she go off looking for another mate? I didn't think so. Pop said coyotes mate for life.

I stood with my shoulder against an oak tree and the wind throwing my hair into my face. I listened for the howl of a coyote or the pad of their feet, but the leaves were banging around in the tree, and the grass was scraping and chiming, and the bedframe that somebody had set over one of the graves was humming in harmony with the wind, and it occurred to me that this might be the kind of night when you see a ghost, and then I told myself not to think about that. Of course, telling yourself not to think about ghosts is a surefire way to think about them. So I was standing, leaning on the tree, thinking hard not about ghosts, becoming aware of changes in the humming of the bedframe, sort of moaning, sort of groaning like a voice from deep underground, from a coffin, maybe, full of dust and bones, dust and bones and teeth, a skull with empty eyesockets — when something cold and wet presses against the back of my knee. I fly forward and jump around.

There stands Miss Arool with a squirrel in her mouth. She wags her tail — just once — she's shy. Hesitantly, two steps forward and one step back, ready to turn tail and flee if I make a sudden move, she steps closer, closer to me until she's directly at my feet. She looks up at me with those wild burning eyes. Then gently she lays the squirrel on the grass. She looks up at me once more. It's a gift. The squirrel is a thank you — thanks for the help.

I whisper: "You're welcome."

She slinks backwards a few steps. She cocks her head sideways, studying me, trying to decide for once and for all whether I'm some strange kind of big coyote or just some other strange kind of small human being.

Suddenly she blinks. And just as suddenly, she turns — runs — and is gone.

"What about the General?" I shout after her.

The only answer is wind.

* * *

Another day passed. After school I knocked on doors and got a job sweeping redwood duff off a man's roof and then cleaning out his gutters.

I built a campfire outside the trailer. I was roasting a couple hot dogs on coat hangers, singing Oh give me a home where the buffalo roam — but there ain't no buffalo around San Puerco — when I hear a car stop at the top of the driveway out of sight. A minute later, here comes Pop. Walking behind him is a woman wearing blue jeans and a straw hat.

"Hi Danny," Pop says, casual, like he's just coming home from a trip to the store.

"Hi," I say. Part of me wants to jump up and hug him. Another part of me wants to jump up and slug him. I guess they fight each other to a draw, because I don't do either. I stay sitting by the fire.

Pop looks like he isn't sure what to do with me, either — whether to hug me, or shake my hand, or just act casual.

"Who you been staying with?" Pop asks.

"Nobody."

"Nobody? Tommy said somebody was taking care of you."

"Somebody was. Me."

"You mean Tommy lied to me?"

"No, Pop. I lied to Tommy."

"You mean you stayed here all by yourself?"

"Not all. There was a couple coyotes."

Pop studies me for a minute. Then he says, "Them coyotes must've done a good job. You look bigger. Taller. Skinny, but tall. You been growing while I was gone?"

"I been okay."

Pop turns to the woman and waves his hand at the trailer. "Well, this is it," he says.

"Don't you have a stove?" she says.

"We're out of propane," I say. I pull a hot dog off a coat hanger. "Want one?"

"No thanks." She bends down so she's on a level with where I'm sitting by the fire. "My name is Carla," she says.

"Hi," I say.

"I'm very pleased to meet you, Danny," she says.

She ain't acting like Pop's usual girlfriends. They don't bend down to talk to me. Or say they're pleased to meet me.

"That looks like fun, cooking on an open fire," she says.

"It gets the job done," I say.

"Carla's a nurse," Pop says. "I met her in the hospital. We got to be friends."

At least she had a job. That was an improvement over Pop's usual friends.

"Carla's moving," Pop says. "She just found a place in town. I'm going to help her move tomorrow."

Carla's still bent down so she's on my level by

the campfire. She says, "I've heard a lot about you, Danny. Your father is very proud of you. He says you're a wonderful soccer player."

"Who, me?" I say. I never knew Pop bragged about me.

"He also says that you like to play poker." She grinned. "So do I. Maybe we could all play a game some time. After I get moved into my new house."

Pop interrupts: "Say — is that my jacket you're wearing, Danny?"

"Yes, sir." Where I'm sitting, he can't see the writing on back; otherwise, he'd know for sure. "Sorry," I say, and I start to slip it off.

"Keep it," Pop says. "That's all right. I'm done with it."

Pop and Carla exchange a look. Carla smiles.

I slip the jacket back up on my shoulders.

"Well, thanks for the ride," Pop says to Carla.

"Talk to you later, Danny," Carla says. She follows Pop up the driveway. A minute later, I hear a car start. Coming back to the trailer, Pop looks around and shakes his head. "Look at this dump," he says. "I know she wanted to look inside, but I was too embarrassed to show it to her."

"It's all right," I say. I remember Law looking around in the trailer. He thought it was neat.

"Look at that television." Pop says. "I can't believe I shot it."

"You were nuts, Pop."

Pop shakes his head. "I was angry." He takes a

deep breath in, then blows it out. He says, "I felt like nobody could understand how angry I was. Nobody. But something I found out in the hospital was lots of people feel the same way. It helps to talk about it. That's practically all we did was talk."

"About the war?"

"That. And the system."

"What system?"

"The whole system that makes you go to war. It's nuts, Danny. The whole system is nuts — not the people who fight in it. Though it makes them nuts, too, I guess. So we got together. I talked. They talked. Some of them had much bigger problems than me. At least I've got all my arms and legs — even my fingers and toes."

"So you're not angry any more?"

"I'm still angry." Pop frowns. "I'll always be."

"I'm glad you're home, Pop."

"Home? This is home? This is a dump. I want to move to town."

"Town? Which town?"

"San Puerco. The busy metropolis." He laughs.

Good. I was afraid he might want to move over the hill to Pulgas Park where I don't know anybody. But I should've known. Pop likes the mountains, where everybody's a little bit different — or, some people, a whole lot different — a little wild, a little crazy, a little bit of coyote in us all.

*   *   *

In the morning I'm eating jelly doughnuts when Pop comes out of his room in a T-shirt and undershorts and sits down across from me at the table.

"Funny thing happened last night, after you were asleep," Pop says. "I thought I heard a noise outside. I look out the window, and there's this coyote on the front steps."

"Really? How many legs?"

Pop looks at me funny. "Four," he says. "What'd you expect? Six?"

"If it was four, that was Miss Arool."

"You know her? Well, maybe that explains it. She had a squirrel in her mouth. She lays that squirrel down on the top step, then she backs off. I open the door. She takes one look at me, and she's gone like a puff of smoke."

"And she left the squirrel?"

"It's still there. Now what's that all about?"

"It's a gift. Like a thank you."

"Thanks for what?"

"I helped her partner after he got caught in a trap. I sort of nursed him a little bit."

"A little bit of nursing can be a fine thing," Pop says, and he reaches for a jelly doughnut.

At school I rounded up volunteers, and after school we all went to Carla's cabin where she and Pop were unloading boxes from a U-Haul truck.

Boone, Babcock, Law, and Geraldine all pitched in with me to help.

I saw right away that Law didn't have a clue about how to move things. I'd never realized there was anything to know until I watched Law try to push a trunk by himself that should have had three people carrying it, and then when Boone and I helped him, Law got picked off trying to fit through a door sideways. But he kept trying, and he got the hang of it — after all, there isn't much to learn, and Law learns fast.

Carla picked up some pizzas and sodas. Babcock gobbled a whole pizza himself. Then he went home for his diet dinner. Watching him reminded me of how hungry I'd been, and how glad I was not to be hungry anymore, and how crazy it is for people to make themselves hungry on *purpose*, and how sorry I feel now for kids who never get enough to eat.

Boone and Law said they had to go home, too. Geraldine picked some flowers, and Carla put them in some soda cans with water. Boxes were piled everywhere. Carla unpacked a radio and turned on some music. Pop pushed some boxes together to make a table, and Carla unpacked a deck of cards and some poker chips.

"You ever play poker, Geraldine?" I asked.

"No. Is it hard?"

Good, I was thinking. At least here's one person I can beat.

We played for just a half hour before Geraldine lost all her chips. We each gave her some of ours.

"We should quit, soon," Carla said.

"Let's go for broke," I said.

Pop didn't say anything. But he stood up and walked around his chair. Well, I knew what he was up to, so I stood up and walked around my chair, too. Pop glared at me. Carla and Geraldine didn't move, so I knew they couldn't win. It would be a test to see whose luck was stronger — mine or Pop's. Geraldine dealt. We were playing five-card draw, deuces and one-eyed jacks wild. I bid every chip I had. Pop pushed out every chip he had. Carla and Geraldine did the same.

"Well, what you got?" Pop said.

Carla showed her hand: two pair — two tens and two eights.

"Got you," Pop said, and he showed two queens and a deuce.

"Does that mean you have three of a kind?" Geraldine asked. "Three queens?"

"Yep," Pop said. "I win."

"No, you don't," I said. I laid down my ace, deuce, and one-eyed jack.

Pop slammed his hand on the table. "Beginner's luck," he snarled.

"Is that the same as three aces?" Geraldine asked.

"Exactly," I said. I put my arms around all the chips to sweep them over to my side of the table.

Meanwhile, Geraldine slowly set down her cards. "You guys are so lucky," she said. "All I had was three sevens. And this silly pair of fours." Then her lips turned up in a sly smile, and she broke into a grin.

Full house. Geraldine won. And Carla looked pleased for her. I think Carla was feeling like she had a new full house, too.

Pop told me I'd better run along home now. He said he wanted to stay a while and help Carla some more.

I knew better than to ask any questions. Geraldine walked out with me. The sun was gone, but there was still light in the sky.

"Going home?" Geraldine said.

"Later," I said, "First I'm going to a graveyard."

"Looking for ghosts?"

"Hope not. Hope he's still alive."

"Who?"

"A coyote."

"Can I come?"

Without talking, we walked up the road, over the fence to the little graveyard at the top of the hill under a deep purple sky.

Geraldine sat on a tombstone. "Who's buried here?" she asked.

"I don't know."

"Do coyotes come here?"

"Sometimes."

"Danny? Remember once when Dylan tried to

kiss me, and I gave him a bloody nose?"

"I remember."

"I just want you to know, I wouldn't do that to *everybody*."

"Good thing," I said. "Because somebody else, they might hit you *back*."

I turned my back to Geraldine and leaned my shoulder against the tree. The last light was fading. Where are you, General Mess? Did you crawl off in some hole to die?

Geraldine came to the tree and leaned her shoulder against the other side.

"We're moving," I said. "Pop wants to move back to town. To San Puerco."

"Oh. That'll be good," Geraldine said. "Don't you think so?"

"Some ways, yes."

"Do you think he'll move in with Carla? Do you think they'll get married? Do you like Carla? I do."

"I like her," I said.

I looked out toward the hills. I'd given up on finding General Mess. I was saying good-bye to the fields and all the golden grass waiting for the rains, waiting to turn green once again. Living in town, I won't come out here. Except maybe once in a while, to visit. Good-bye to the cows, sad-eyed and solemn. Good-bye to the sheep, little puffs way off in the distance. Good-bye crickets. Good-bye mice.

I lean back and howl. It's my good-bye song.

Geraldine looks at me like I'm crazy.

Nobody answers.

The wind is blowing the clouds around. The grass bends and straightens, bends and straightens. The rainy season's coming. It'll be nice to be out of the trailer with its leaky roof.

What's that?

I see a gray motion down the hill in the grass. Like a moving shadow. On three legs.

I hold still.

It's General Mess. Looking wobbly on three legs. And he's stalking something. Now he's standing perfectly still with the half leg in front sticking out like it's pointing.

He pounces. He stabs with just the one front paw. He loses his balance, rolls to the side snapping his head, and — got it. A mouse. Between his teeth.

Miss Arool trots up behind him. General Mess cocks his head, showing off his prize. He wags his tail. Miss Arool steps forward and tries to grab it from his mouth with her teeth. The General jerks it away. But he wants it to be a game. He stands there, head cocked, and Arool lunges again. She's got her teeth on it. The General holds on. They play tug-of-war until suddenly the General loses his balance, and Arool jerks her head away with the prize.

The General falls into a heap.

Arool sidles up to him and drops the mouse where he can grab it. The General stands up, looking a little grouchy now, and takes the mouse a few steps away. And eats it.

I look at Geraldine. I'm smiling. I don't know when I took it, but I'm holding her hand. Geraldine is gaping at the coyotes with a look of wonder. I don't think we moved, but I guess we made a sound because suddenly both coyotes are looking our way. They raise their noses in the air. The way the wind is blowing, I don't think they can smell us.

No matter. They're spooked and already they're trotting away. The General has a hobbling three-legged gait. For balance, he jerks his tail with each hop. He's getting the hang of how to live with a limp.

I tilt back my head for one last howl. This one ain't to say good-bye. It's hello. Hello, world, look out for Danny.

Here I come, strong as grass.

ABOUT THE AUTHOR

Joe Cottonwood lives in La Honda, California. He is forty-four years old, has been married for over twenty years, and has three children. He makes his living repairing and remodeling houses as a licensed general contractor. For relaxation, he makes bread.

Danny Ain't is a companion book to *The Adventures of Boone Barnaby* (Scholastic Hardcover, 1990), the author's first novel about the adventures of three friends in the small town of San Puerco, in the Santa Cruz Mountains of California.